Two Sisters

Two Sisters

Sam Cutrufelli Sr.

ReadersMagnet, LLC

Two Sisters
Copyright © 2023 by *Sam Cutrufelli Sr.*

Published in the United States of America
ISBN   Paperback: 978-1-957312-72-9
ISBN   eBook: 978-1-957312-73-6

All rights reserved. No part of this publication may be reproduced, stored in a retrieval system or transmitted in any way by any means, electronic, mechanical, photocopy, recording or otherwise without the prior permission of the author except as provided by USA copyright law.

The opinions expressed by the author are not necessarily those of ReadersMagnet, LLC.

ReadersMagnet, LLC
10620 Treena Street, Suite 230 | San Diego, California, 92131 USA
1.619. 354. 2643 | www.readersmagnet.com

Book design copyright © 2023 by ReadersMagnet, LLC. All rights reserved.

Cover design by Ericka Obando
Interior design by Dorothy Lee

VII

Sam Cutrufelli, Sr.

My name is Jacqulyn Montage, and you might say, so what? It's not a household name or even an inspirational name, but it is what it is. This morning I attended a funeral as my father passed on yesterday and it left a financial void that wasn't there twenty-four hours ago. I was the oldest in the family — fifteen years old to be exact. I had a responsibility to my younger sister who was three years younger. I took off from school to administer to my father so I'm a year behind my peers. While my father was slowly but surely seeing his last days, the two of us, my father and I, would reminisce or just talk. My father was not well educated, let alone a philosopher, but to me he talked sense. He told me that at times life could be brutal, but if I didn't let it get me down, it usually came around for another cycle. My father said that many times. He and my mother had little except their love for each other. My mother called him Dad and she said that if we had a slice of bread and a piece of cheese we would get by. My father was a railroad man so when my mother and father got married, she gave my father a gold railroad watch. In subsequent years, he managed to buy a long gold chain that he fastened to the watch. He would push the little button and the lid would fly out, displaying a white face watch with black numerals. During his last or near last breath, he told me that he was sorry he could not leave me money or property. Life was such that it was elusive for him, but he wanted me to have his gold watch and chain. We both hugged as he handed me the best gift or legacy a person could ever hope for, and he passed on for a better world as this would be the day he would be reunited with the love of his life. For the last year or so, I went to school during the day and at five p.m., I worked a shift as a waitress. The small amount of money I brought in barely covered our expenses, but my sister and I endured. My sister's name was Shelly, and she was a very attractive girl. I was always told that my younger sister was gorgeous and beautiful and that she had everything — a beautiful face, and a beautiful body to match. Sometimes we would get a job at a department store that needed a young pretty model. She would be so proud when she gave me some extra money and it was nice but not often enough to build up a reserve. Now that my father had passed on, it was time for me to make some pertinent decisions.

First, I realized that my capabilities to earn any significant amount of money was not going to happen unless I prepared myself capability-wise. In other words, I had to either get more advanced education or possibly stay in the same rut I am now in. I really didn't believe in a fairy godmother endowing me with a windfall. Well, it was going to be up to me. I had to prepare myself. The first move I had to make was to transfer myself from a purely academic type of school to a trade school of sorts. So, I took the time to go to the city school board and see what they had to offer. I talked to a very nice elderly lady who was introduced as a school counselor. She was very attentive and after listening to my tale of woe she recommended that I transfer to a trade type school that would prepare me to earn a degree in secretarial or art or sewing. They even had a rudimental course on nursing. I agreed so she had me fill out a form and just that quick, I was enrolled in a secretarial course. I started this semester about fifteen days late, so I had a lot of catching up to do. I did not have a typewriter of my own and even if I did, I worked my waitress job at night so all in all, my time was well used up. After a few days of getting acquainted, a shy Chinese girl said that she saw that I was behind and with my permission, she would like to help me catch up. That was a gift from heaven. So, I told her that

I went to school all day and worked nights as a waitress. She was not bothered and said that I had Saturday and Sunday, and that I could come as much as my brain would absorb. "I have a typewriter and some blank secretary books. With your permission I'll be at your home Saturday morning at seven a.m. Please have the coffee brewing. I'm a real taskmaster and I'll work your butt off," she said.

May Wong said the first thing she needed was my address and we both started giggling. Sure enough, Saturday at fifteen to seven a.m, May rang the bell, announcing her arrival. I opened the door and almost collapsed. In the driveway was a brand-new red convertible. May said it belonged to her brother who was at college, and he gave her the okay to use the car. So, May drove. I never was behind the wheel of a car, let alone even ridden in many cars before. So, May lived up to her promise as a taskmaster and we accomplished a lot. She showed me how to position my hands over the keyboard. After eight hours of grueling work, May said she had to leave, but would be back tomorrow. She also left her typewriter so that I could practice at my leisure. Sunday was a repeat of Saturday and May complimented me on my progress and she said I had a mind like a sponge. Where did such wonderful people come from? Monday to Friday of the second week was easier than Saturday and Sunday. I was well caught up with some of the laggard in the class. In fact, one boy asked me for some advice. Imagine me giving advice. After I caught up, it was easy. I excelled at shorthand; typing was not my strongest forte, but I was still above average. The school semester was nearing its final days. So, we had to sign up for next semester and the secretary courses were for two semesters. Thanks to May, I was well on my way to becoming an accredited member of the office work force. Incidentally, I had not seen May for two weeks and I assumed that she took some time off as she was well ahead of everyone in the class. I called her parents, but the mother answered, and she only spoke Chinese. When I first met May, she gave me a list of relatives and their phone numbers. So, I started calling.

The father did not answer. So, I called the father's sister. The sister was very polite and apologetic that May did not tell her what was going on. The sister said that May was in a tuberculosis hospital in Chicago, undergoing a series of tests. "Please write to her as she is probably lonely."

So, I got the address and wrote to May. I thanked her for all her kindness and diligence and told her that without her help I never would have made it. On a more serious note, I asked her what the matter was and how serious it was. I had the scary thought that it was very serious. May returned my letter with a letter of her own. It read, "Dear Jacqulyn, in the very short time that I have known you, you have been very dear to me. I miss you very much. My prognosis is not very good. In fact, to be frank with you, I do not have very much time left — probably two weeks. Please write again for your letters are special to me. Thank you, Jacqulyn, for the poignant letter. As you read on, you will note the big tears on the paper. It is not a tear of despair or of my being afraid, but it is a tear of my friendship for you and what I am going to miss. Thank you again, Jacqulyn for the brief but everlasting friendship we developed."

A few days later I received a letter from May's brother, Richard Wong, and he said May had passed away on Tuesday, June twelfth which was two days ago. "She was very weak and tired. If I can remember, May never had a friend until you came along," said her brother. "Thank you, Jacqulyn, for making her happy," signed Richard Wong.

I graduated from school; I was seventeen years old. I decided to take a week off and just bask in the admiration for the task that I accomplished. The next day I went strolling through the park and I spotted a deserted bench or almost deserted as there was an old man sitting on one end of the bench. So, I sat on the opposite end. There was a trash can alongside the bench, and I could see a nicely rolled up newspaper, but I did not want to retrieve it because the old man might not think it was very feminine to do so. Suddenly, he tapped the bench with his cane, and he told me I could have his fresh newspaper. He also remarked that the only reason for his buying the paper was to see the horse race results. Then he said, "Bah! I never win. All I do is feed the beast." He handed me the paper and went limping off.

When he got out of sight, I opened the paper to the help-wanted section and there were six ads, one for an auto mechanic that must have his own tools. A department store had an ad, but I fell for that gimmick before. All they wanted was a catalog of potential names if the economy got better. *Just fill out this application. We will review some and notify you later. Thank you.* The second from the last ad read 'apprentice office help wanted, call this number,' but it had no address. So, I reached in my purse and got out my gold pen and pencil set and a piece of notepaper. I wrote the number down and carefully laid the paper down for someone else to read. Before I left, I ate my peanut butter and jelly sandwich that I had in my purse, plus half of a delicious apple. The other half was for Shelly's lunch. Off I went to look for a phone and dialed the number. A man answered and I told him that I saw his ad and would like an address. He gave me the address, but I could not quite get it. He said it was on Main Street — such and such number — and hung up. I surely was not going to squander another coin. I would just walk down Main Street until I saw the shop as the man said it was a perfumery.

It worked like a charm. It was about six blocks from the bench. There it was: Princess and Perfume, and Scents was the name of the shop. I opened the door and walked in. A bell announced my presence, and a young man came from behind a three fourth high partition and all he said was, "You called?" I said yes. The young man said he would get me an application. Then he said I was young, and I said I was older than I was yesterday, and he started laughing so I started laughing, too. He said that was a good one and left to get the application. I filled it out and left.

A squatty looking man with a white mustache ran to get the door before it slammed shut. The mustache man was the owner of Princess Perfume. He walked into the small office. George Plum greeted him and said that he had two responses to the ad. Mr. Rock, the owner, said, "Good. Did you test them?"

George had a hard time trying to evade the question. Finally he blurted out some silly reason for not testing the two applicants.

"No go." Mr. Rock threw up his arms and said, "You know, George, you are my nephew but at times you are just impossible. You know that Mabel is leaving for her two-week vacation soon and who the hell do you think is going to answer the phone? Send out the statements, and of course do some shorthand letters. Okay, the damage is done; we ran the ad for one week and we got two results and you blew it. Get on the damn phone and get them back in here."

So, George got belligerent and said, "I told you that they both had experience, so I figured that we didn't have to test them."

"You're a good chemist but you sure are naive. If they told you they were the Queen of Sheba, you would believe them. Of course, they would say they are competent and why do you think they answered the ad? Do you have their telephone numbers? Yes, okay, so get on it."

George called the first applicant and she said she had office experience but did not specify as to the extent. She answered the phone and George who was still steaming said, "Get down here now and take a typing test."

The lady was indignant and said he could ram his job and hung up. So, he called the second girl who he thought was too young, but on her application, she said she had just graduated from secretarial school and was proficient in typing and shorthand. Jacqulyn's sister answered the phone. This time George was not so brisk, and he respectively told Shelly that he would like for Jacqulyn to please come to the office. He fibbed a little and said that she was one of the applicants they were considering. Could she come in today? Jacqulyn came home about an hour later and Shelly told her about the request. So Jacqulyn hurried to the Princess office. When she got there, George, the young man she talked to earlier was out to lunch, but Mr. Rock was there.

Jacqulyn introduced herself and said that she got a call to come in for a test. Mr. Rock was on the defensive. Soon they would be getting applicants just out of diapers, heck she was only three fourths his age or, for that matter, Mabel's age. He composed himself and introduced himself. He then asked her if she could type out a prepared paragraph or two that was supposed to determine if the typist was qualified. The two paragraphs covered most of what would be needed in a small retail type market. It had colons, commas, explanation points, plus some big words and small words. It was a comprehensive test and if the applicantpassed it, it was assumed that she had whatever it took to work as a secretary. When Jacqulyn was in school, they tested on the same two paragraphs many times, so Jacqulyn passed the typing test like a pro. Mr. Rock was impressed as he thought to himself, *this young girl has it all together.*

"Now, Miss, I am going to read you some sentences from this book. Would you please use your shorthand with what I have read to you?" So, Mr. Rock began reading slowly at first and then picking up the pace, so Jacqulyn had to decipher faster.

Again it was easy for Jacqulyn as she passed all her shorthand tests in school with above A marks. She was hired on the spot.

"Come in tomorrow at eight a.m. and be prepared to help Mabel who has been with us for over five years. You will be her assistant. Thank you, Miss, and see you tomorrow."

Shortly thereafter, George walked into the office. Mr. Rock grabbed his hand and with a big smile said, "Good work, George.

So now what's the old guy up to?" *Two hours ago, I was trash now I'm filet mignon.*

Jacqulyn stopped at a market on her way home and bought an apple pie, Shelly's favorite, and a pint of vanilla ice cream. Celebration time was on the horizon. She told Shelly what had happened, and she was hired on the spot. Jacqulyn was beside herself as she kept patting herself on the back until Shelly said if she broke her arm, she probably would not have a job. They both ate pie a la mode like two excited little girls. When they were stuffed, they both agreed that it had been a long time since they enjoyed such a treat. The next day couldn't come fast enough for Jacqulyn. as she looked at the clock at five a.m., then again at five ten a.m.. She thought maybe the clock was broken so she went to her purse and took out her father's railroad watch. It read five twelve a.m. — nope, the clocks were okay. Time crawled by slowly but surely towards seven a.m. . . . . . Seven a.m. was the time she had to leave to get to work on time as she decided to walk to work.

When she arrived at the office, she was introduced to Mrs. Rock and again to George. Mabel had to drop in early to get something so Jacqulyn was introduced to her also. Mabel said her goodbyes and wished Jacqulyn the best of luck and she was gone. Later that day, as she was chatting with Mrs. Rock, Mr. Rock said that Mabel was going on a vacation for two weeks and she said that Jacqulyn was the prime secretary, and they both laughed. As it ended up, Jacqulyn and Mrs. Rock got on exceptionally well and Mrs. Rock told her husband that if she had a child, she would wish it to be just like Jacqulyn. Mr. Rock liked Jacqulyn, so he was the one who introduced her to her tasks. While he was at it, he told Jacqulyn that the chemist and office help did not get a paid vacation the first year, but they did the following year. The second year, it was two weeks with pay and sometimes a bonus was thrown in. So, Mr. Rock showed Jacquelyn the inbox and outbox and explained that the outbox brought in the money as it was where the statements-to-customers books are. In this case, there were about fifteen statements to be sent out. Mr. Rock said it was imperative to always keep up with the statements as that was what kept the office doors open.

Jacqulyn's first day at the office went by at the speed of lightning. She was still at her desk when Mr. Rock asked her if she was going to spend the night there. Of course, he was kidding. The Rocks lived on the outskirts of the city, so they drove each day. Mrs. Rock asked Jacqulyn if they could drop her off somewhere. Jacquelyn said she would walk to the restaurant that employed her since she was fourteen years old. The restaurant was coincidentally on the same street as Princess Perfume and only six blocks apart. It was situated across the park that she now dubbed "lucky park" with the lucky park bench as that was where the old racehorse man gave her the newspaper that featured the ad that led her to the job at Princess Perfume. The restaurant employed an elderly lady who was the dishwasher. She also cleared tables. She drove to work each day and she went right past the small apartment where Jacqulyn and her sister lived. So, Jacqulyn always got a ride home at night which was a blessing because at fourteen years old, a girl out at ten p.m. in the evening was fair game to come to all sorts of sinister happenings. She was lucky, very lucky. Time flew by, I guess, mainly because Jacqulyn loved her job so much and of course everyone who worked at Princess Perfume adored Jacqulyn. Again, she felt blessed that what was happening to her was indeed reality.

Mabel, the bookkeeper and secretary, came back from her two-week vacation and after a brief settling in, Jacqulyn's workload lightened considerably. To be honest, Mr. Rock's intentions were to hire a secretary to fill in for Mabel and then dismiss her as was the program each year when Mabel went on vacation. This time it was different. Jacqulyn was in their blood and was there to stay. Jacqulyn knew that she was dispensable if push came to shove. So, she proposed to Mr. and Mrs. Rock that maybe on a slack day she could contact the local department stores that carried Princess products. Again, Jacqulyn was lucky as the plan brought in a good number of extra sales. In fact, department stores called Mr. Rock and thanked him for sending Jacqulyn.

"Your product was kind of pushed to the side as there were more popular label perfumes for sale. That pretty girl was unfazed, and she dusted all the bottles off, and she took the time to set up small displays, and she took the time to sales pitch all the cosmetic girls. She told them that there were perfumes that were overrated and if they pushed the qualities of Princess Perfume, it would be a win-win situation for both as the cosmetic girls were on salary and commission and their paycheck would show an increase as their sales increased. Fortunately for the store, we were able to sell more perfume, the girls did better, and consequently you did better."

It was true. Sales were picking up. Customers who placed an order were now calling in orders at an amazing rate. Mabel loved Jacqulyn and wished she had a daughter like her although it was wishful thinking. There was no harm in wishful thinking. Mabel was getting on in years so she delegated more and more of her responsibilities to Jacqulyn. She also proposed to Mr. Rock a decrease in her work time as she would like to work four days a week rather than five days, as her husband also was on a four-day work schedule. She told Mr. Rock that Jacqulyn was more than qualified to handle the workload. So, Fridays, Jacqulyn was the senior secretary even if it was only for a day.

For Jacqulyn to get ahead of it, she worked a split shift on Saturday and Sunday at the restaurant. She came in at seven a.m. and worked until noon, then returned for her normal evening shift. Occasionally Mr. and Mrs. Rock would go to the Princes Perfume store and tidy up or finish some work. When they did, they would come to Jacqulyn's restaurant and have brunch as they knew that Jacqulyn got off at noon. When the Rocks came in to eat, for Jacqulyn, it was like the King and Queen of England came in to eat at her station. She adored both as much as they adored her.

Jacqulyn was on her second year at Princess Perfume. Mabel was not doing too well and she was now working three days a week. Mabel and her husband did not need the money that badly as Mabel's husband was a senior bookkeeper at a worldwide oil corporation. His salary was more than adequate so Mabel did not have to work. But like so many people that worked all their lives, she knew that boredom would set in, and she didn't think she could handle that very well.

The other change that came about at Princess Perfume was that she and George were becoming a twosome. Eventually George and Jacqulyn got married. She was now twenty years old, and George was two years older. Her sister, Shelly, was now seventeen years old and would graduate from high school this term. Married life was a boon to George as he worked hard and did not chase around and did not drink excessively so Jacqulyn thought she had a winner. The second year went into the third year. That's when her life got uprooted again. Jacqulyn's life was never a steady course. For as long as she could remember, it always, always had its ups and downs, mostly downs. The two or three years she worked for Mr. and Mrs. Rock at the perfume shop were the best years of her life to date but that changed abruptly for the staff at Princess Perfume. Here are the gory details.

The last day anyone would work again at Princess Perfumes went on as usual, but that evening was never to be forgotten although no one from the Princess staff witnessed anything but the aftermath and destruction.

The actual catastrophe began about eight years ago. Mr. and Mrs. Rock were, at that time, self-employed chemists. They were both licensed chemists who had elected to be self-employed. At a small laboratory that was part of a large laboratory, they performed many routine chemical analyses for firms that did not have a chemical staff. The food industry was the biggest profit-making part of their operation. Although others began to shine like the perfume and scent industry, they usually had their own chemistry people. So, Mr. and Mrs. Rock experimented with perfumes and scents because they thought it was a worthy option to pursue. Eventually, through trial-and-error, Mr. and Mrs. Rock thought they had a winner perfume. So, they decided to mortgage the farm so to speak and set up what was now Princess Perfume and Scent Company. They had to start from scratch — order bottles that were attractive, order special labels. They also had to purchase equipment, glues for the labels. Although they had a rudimentary supply of assorted office equipment, they now knew this new venture had very different needs. So, while the Rocks were busy with the one aspect of opening a new business, they also had to find larger quarters that could satisfy them for at least five years. They heard of a single-story building on Main Street that was for lease. They inquired and concluded that this would work. The building was represented as a single story, street level property. There was a basement that was as large as the footprint of the street floor level. The basement was nicely complemented into two sections — one was a smaller office space incidentally and was coincidentally occupied by three chemists who worked along the same lines that the Rock's had been doing previously through their ongoing venture into the perfume business. The other section was much larger and was used as a card room. Each unit had a set of concrete steps that went to the street. So, they were set. The name of the venture was Princess Perfumes and Scents Company — named after Mrs. Rock who had a little American Indian blood in her. As everyone knows, almost all Indian girls were Princesses, so Mr. Rock called Mrs. Rock: Princess Rock.

Everything after that hurdle went smoothly. The building they leased was partitioned as the Rocks thought this to be ample for their needs. The laboratory took up about one-third of the space as that would be the moneymaking end. The office and waiting room took up another one- third space. The office space was central, and the other third was for storage and warehouse.

The laboratory was the most expensive part of the program as it had to have gas lines for the Bunsen burners and plumbing for sinks and some refrigeration. Although they had some of the supplies, they had nowhere near what was estimated as needed for they had a porcelain steel table that allowed ample space to accommodate three chemists working simultaneously at the same table. The table had three gas lines, one for each chemist. The Rocks were very conservative about what they were getting into, and were scared. Mrs. Rock came up with a simple plan that was to help keep them afloat. She suggested that they do not eliminate the type of work they were doing for the last three years as they already had a built-in clientele in a cash flow coming in each month. Sometimes it is wrong to try to run two different types of operations as you make here and lose there but, in this case, they both agreed they were both along the same lines. Only one business would be subletting to potential customers and the perfume business would be out in a venture to be established — no easy tasks as there were many competitive perfumes on the market from expensive to cheap, as you might buy in a five and dime store. So, they blindly groped with much trial and error and they were rewarded with a very saleable product. The Princess line of perfumes was middle of the line, so it had a better exposure potential than say, a worldwide label. Things were looking up slowly but surely. George, Mr. Rock's nephew, graduated as a chemist and he became the number three chemist at the firm. Seeing that George was recently graduated, the Rocks thought he might be more attuned to the rapid changes in the food business, so they let George handle most of the type of business that were previously invested in. Mr. and Mrs. Rock concentrated on the perfume end. It worked out well. In fact, George brought in more money than the perfume operation. All in all, they were well pleased. Mrs. Rock bought a home course of bookkeeping and office work, and she did fine with it. But one day, she got fed up and told Mr. Rock that she was not going to do book work. So that morning, she had some ideas along the chemistry lines. Mr. Rock sputtered and had a fit. He said it was imperative that she do the book work because there would be quite a bit of money coming in. That's when she blew up. She said, "Dear Mr. Rock, I am not a feminist but if you think for one minute that just because I am a woman, I can be stereotyped, you are mistaken. Furthermore, take off your dirty old apron and as fast as your legs can carry you, go to the newspaper office and have them put an ad in for a part time bookkeeper. When you get someone, I don't ever want to see ink on my fingers again. After all, I'm a chemist — as good or better than your old boy. In fact, while you're doing that, on your way back. bring me a chocolate shake."

Well, Mr. Rock was aghast, but he knew when to keep his mouth shut so he took it out on George. "Listen, George, I am going to tidy up for a while so go get Mrs. Rock her milkshake. Yes, chocolate."

The next day, Mabel came in and she said she was ready to work. Mabel was about forty years old, and she was loud. If there was a crowd, you could always hear Mabel's voice above the others. So, the two Rocks were bamboozled by this arrogant bookkeeper whom after a short stint, they knew that they could not get along without. There was nothing she would not do but nobody dared order her to do it. She would just as soon tell them to shove it, as Mrs. Rock told Mr. Rock. Well, every office has a gossiper and George was it. He told Mabel what happened yesterday and the reason she was there. Mabel went up to Mrs. Rock and gave her a big hug and said good for her.

One day, the chemist in the basement left his Bunsen burner on accidentally. It was later determined that the chemistry business that they were allegedly doing was just a front for the illicit drugs that they were pumping out. That night, there was a leak out of a tank of meth and about three a.m., it exploded when the stuff contacted the burner. The explosion was catastrophic, and a raging fire developed that destroyed Princess Perfume. The floor of Princess collapsed and ended up in the basement as did the roof and sides. It was a total disaster that was more than the fire crews could cope with. No one was hurt or killed as it was three a.m. Mr. and Mrs. Rock were called and all they could do was hug each other silently and weep.

The next day, the newspapers had a field day. The district attorney's office said it was investigating but they already knew the fire was centered in just the workshop and they were making illicit drugs. The District Attorney went on to say that they would indict Mr. and Mrs. Rock as owners of Princess Perfume for obstruction of justice as they were familiar with the operation in the basement but did not tell the authorities. Mr. and Mrs. Rock told the reporters vehemently that they knew nothing of the operation below them. They said that they knew many chemists but did not know these three men. If they met on the street, they would not say hello and continue their path. Never once did they associate with each other, but the damage was done, and Mr. Rock's insurance would not pay on the policy until the investigation or future development came up from the district attorney's office. Mr. Rock hired attorneys, but they were ignored until such time when the case would go to trial. The three basement chemists were arrested and out on bail. It was a futile attempt for the district attorney's office to try to conceal the ineptness of the legal system for not realizing the illicit action going on for four or five years right under their noses. They tried to find a scapegoat in Mr. and Mrs. Rock. They tried to imply that Princess Perfumes was also a front for illicit purposes. The explosion was well over six months ago and Mr. and Mrs. Rock were at a standstill. They needed the insurance money to relocate. The banks were not willing to loan because of the pending court case. George was out of work, as well as Jacqulyn and Mabel. Of the three, only Mabel was able to survive because her husband commanded a good salary. George and Jacqulyn both worked for Princess Perfume but that was now defunct and they had no income.

George was kind of blackballed because of the allegations and Jacqulyn could not find any secretarial work as there was none.

Jacqulyn and George were hard pressed. Jacqulyn managed to get four hours of work at the restaurant on day shift. Her work in the evenings kept them barely above water. George had no love for banks, and he did not have a bank account. The little money he had above his salary was in his wallet. Jacqulyn did not have the same inclinations for she always had a bank account since she worked at the restaurant. That was a saving grace for a while as George started drinking and playing around with women and playing cards all day and night. He literally gave up. So, the money he had stashed was quickly consumed. One day, George said he was leaving town as there was work in California. So, he left and that was the last she ever heard from George. Mr. and Mrs. Rock never heard from George again.

Eventually, Jacqulyn would file for divorce for right now, she needed every cent to live. Jacqulyn's and Shelly's mother had a sister, but she was always in Europe with one or another stage group. She got herself pregnant awhile back and vowed that her child would be born in America. She came back to America to have her child, but there were problems and she had to have a Caesarean operation. The child came out of this unscathed, but the mother had complications and died. The child was adopted by a family that also tragically had a fatal head-on automobile accident that killed both her adopted parents. She happened to be at a picnic with some friends, so she was probably saved. Now she was the same age as Jacqulyn, and she was very well-off as she inherited the home and other securities that her mother had. Somehow, she got wind of Jacqulyn's problems with the explosion, and she wrote Jacqulyn. It eventually led to the fact that she then asked Shelly to come and visit her in Washington D.C. where her adopted father worked as a lawyer for the state department. She thought that maybe she could help Shelly get some modeling work or actress gigs. That did not last long as Melissa was a party girl and was intoxicated most days and nights with alcohol and drugs. Shelly asked Melissa for money to ride the bus home, but she was always out and that she apparently couldn't come up with a coherent reason. Shelly wanted to leave. So, she told Shelly there was money in the drawers in between the mattress so *get your money and leave, you ungrateful whore.* Shelly did just that. She called the Greyhound bus line and was told what it would cost for a one-way ticket. There was money everywhere, but Shelly only took what she needed for her fare and some food. She left a note and thanked her, but she did not mention the money as Melissa was a very sarcastic person and she might try to say that Shelly stole the money. It was getting harder and harder for Jacqulyn to make ends meet as the restaurant was not doing well due to recession. Shelly got an occasional modeling job with the department stores.

Jacqulyn and Shelly lived in the same house all their lives. The mother and father, before they were born, had rented all these years and now Jacqulyn was having trouble paying the rent, so they asked Jacqulyn and Shelly to move out because a relative needed the home. Sometimes you get a break. In this case, it came about from one of her customers. He always had pasta at Jacqulyn's station, and he knew her from the time she was fourteen years old and worked as a waitress. It was slow and Jacqulyn and Marco talked a little. Jacqulyn blurted out that she would be house hunting tomorrow. Marco said she could live in the empty bakery which was very close to the restaurant. Further talk revealed he owned the home next to the bakery and he owned the bakery building as well. Marco sold his home and was leaving for Italy in about a week. Marco gave Jacqulyn a key and told her to go look at it. Jacqulyn said she did not need an address because she went into the bakery many times, so she knew where it was. The owner of the bakery was a German called Herman. He and his wife ran the place. He also sold bakery goods to the restaurant where she worked. When Jacqulyn went to the bakery, Herman always said, "you no pay." Marco said that Herman was his last name. The Hermans had one bambino and Marco said that bambino was the best baker of the family, but he was not allowed to go into the public area, so he was always in the back, making products. When the parents died, the bakery was closed. The bambino disappeared. It had been closed for over two years. Marco was trying to sell the building but this year, Mr. Right never came along so it remained empty. "Please go look at it," he said and he resumed eating his spaghetti with French bread and a dessert- like canoli or tiramisu.

The next day, Jacqulyn went to the bakery. The two plate glass windows were broken and were boarded up. So, she took the key Marco gave her and she went inside. It was a mess. The retail store was large with showcase encounters all over and there was a separation wall with two doors. The work area was here. There were about eight garbage cans with flour in them. Some had weevils or other flower bugs. Some were moldy. All needed to be thrown out. There were counters with canvas for rolling and there were scales, scoops, mixing bowls, and rolling pins. You name it — it was there. There was nothing electrical, like stand-up mixers or counter mixers. Possibly Marco sold them, or they were stolen. To one side of the workspace was a hole that led to a door and the lock on the door was opened with the same key. Behind the door was a spacious living quarter — old fashioned but it was in good shape. There were two bedrooms with a closet and a kitchen pantry. The only appliance was a wood stove. On the counter was a sink with a window above it and there was a yard. There were two apple trees and a peach tree, and the garden was overgrown with weeds. There was a big living room with linoleum on the floor but no furniture. Off the kitchen was an enclosed porch. All in all, it was a nice. It needed some elbow grease and soap and water, but it did not appear to have any rodents which was surprising. Rodents love flour, but everything in the bakery was in airtight cans. So, she locked up the place and she would talk to Marco when he came in. She went home and had a peanut butter sandwich but she was without apples, so she had a glass of water with the sandwich. Shelly came home shortly and said she was tired of walking, and she was job hunting to no avail as Jacqulyn did not want to tell Shelly about her visit to the former bakery or of her present landlord's request that they move out of the house. Jacqulyn had been protecting Shelly from adversities for as long as she could. They would eat a little dinner that Jacqulyn prepared, and she would go to the restaurant for her evening shift. Of course, she was very anxious this evening as she would be talking to Marco about the empty house. It was kind of funny or ironic that Jacqulyn and Marco had known each other for more than ten years but really did not know each other. Marco was a customer. Jacqulyn did not generally work the day shift and she was not privy to Marco's other appearances at the restaurant. He came in each morning and had a light breakfast. His dinner meal was always the same — spaghetti, wine, French bread. For breakfast, Marco always had coffee and a croissant. Marco also had lunch at the restaurant every day. It was also always the same — a very a large bowl of minestrone soup and French bread and a small glass of wine. So tonight would be a different scenario — an actual business dinner affair. It was going to be a hit and run affair as Jacqulyn's first responsibility was to her customers and her job. Fortunately for her it was not too busy so she could manage Marco's proposal plans and keep the restaurant happy. So, the gist of the conversation was that Marco was selling certain properties and leaving America to go back to Italy. Marco and Jacqulyn had a very long acquaintance, but it was very informal, and she was surprised to learn that Marco was the wealthiest, local citizen. Marco owned all the buildings on the corner of Main Street, just a half a block from the restaurant. He also owned a large department store building on the other corner of Main Street, across the street from the bank building. So, it's true you can't judge a book by its cover. So, Marco decided that he would rent the complete building. He would be selling it to Jacqulyn. Jacqulyn would pay half of the agreed amount for rent and the other half would be applied to the mortgage. The bank on the corner would handle the transaction. Jacqulyn was flabbergasted.

Now, the total amount Marco suggested was less than her present rent and she had the bonus that half would go towards the principal. In a few days she and Shelly would be property owners. Jacqulyn agreed to the arrangement and Marco said that he would have his lawyer draw up the contract as was agreed upon. Jacqulyn was to go to the bank tomorrow at one thirty p.m. and meet with him and the attorney for the official signing.

Marco met with his attorney earlier that morning to brief the attorney as to the terms of the contract. The attorney's name was Sebastian. He and Marco were associates for many years. They could talk to each other as friends and not business-related friends. Sebastian told Marco he was giving this young girl a potential fortune. Marco was not to be deterred.

"Listen Sebastian, you write, and I tell you what to write. You have only dollar signs to everything. I have compassion and more regard for humanity then you. I have known this girl for fourteen years. She has no father, no mother, no relatives, and she was given to raise herself and her baby sister. She never has money; she works only to live and eat at fourteen years old. We were never friends like you and I, Sebastian, but you see, this pretty girl was always very nice and says hello to Marco. So, you write, and I will see you at one thirty p.m. and we sign the papers. I leave tomorrow or the next day, so we have dinner together and you buy."

Jacqulyn could not contain herself. When she got home it was about midnight. She had to wake up Shelly and tell her all about what had happened — about her conversation with Marco and her subsequent visits to the bakery. The biggest most important task was facing most people throughout the world and to have a roof over your head. Once you got over that hurdle, you were not out of the woods, but your remaining obstacles were minimized. Shelly was amazed at the enormity of the tale told to her by her sister. Shelly had no idea. She burst out into torrents of tears and said she loved her more than life. Jacqulyn hugged her and told her to go back to sleep. That was easier said than done. Who could sleep after hearing such momentous news!

The next day, Jacqulyn met Marco and Sebastian at the bank. After signing the papers, Marco kissed Jacqulyn and said, "Now you have a roof."

Jacqulyn held the contract to her breast all the way home. After she left, Sebastian said, "I understand better Marco. You are a good man."

The following day was hectic — mainly cleaning, scrubbing, throwing out trash. Jacqulyn told Shelly that they should concentrate on the living quarters as they would be moving there. That's what was done. The next day was more of the same clean, clean, scrub and scrub. Presently a truck pulled up and two burley guys knocked on the door. Jacqulyn answered and they came to replace the two broken plate glass windows. Jacqulyn was aghast. She told them that she did not order the glass to be replaced but they insisted and showed Jacqulyn the work order and that it was paid in full. It was Marco again. So, she was anxious to see Marco at dinner and thank him and tell him the progress they had made. That evening, there was no Marco. Giovanni, the restaurant owner, gave her a note from Marco saying good luck. Inside were two new one-hundreddollar bills. She never saw Marco again. Occasionally Sebastian would come to the restaurant to have dinner. They would talk and if there was news of Marco, he would tell her, but he heard none. Jacqulyn was ever so grateful for everything that Marco had done for her. She was ever so grateful to have a roof over her and Shelly's heads. So, every day was a challenge because her waitress job only provided so much, and she could never get ahead. Jacqulyn had to admit that it seemed only like things were getting better. For one thing, Shelly seemed to be getting more work.. At the restaurant Jacqulyn noticed that the customers were eating better. Before they ate to exist. Now, they were ordering to enjoy. So, at the end of the meal, it was *what's for dessert tonight, Jacqulyn?* So instead of asking for the bill, the customers were asking for dessert. Jacqulyn saw an increase in her tips which always helped her make ends meet. Well, things were better back again before the explosion. Her tips were for her and Shelly to splurge, maybe a movie, or a dinner out. She loved calamari fritti and always went to this small Italian restaurant that prepared them as she liked. Her restaurant did not serve calamari as the owner thought it was too labor intensive. So, every day whether it was premeditated or accidental, she was always looking for that little extra. One day, she would be knocked down by Sebastian and he would ask her if she could relieve her secretary for a week or so. *Thank you, Lord, for leading me in the right direction*, she thought when she decided to go to secretarial school. Other times she would get a part time job in the restaurant. When certain forces took place, like a sickness or a marriage, Jacqulyn was grateful for the opportunity to get ahead a bit. She liked to walk up and down Main Street to keep in shape as she was still a beautiful woman, and she was going to keep it that way. Timing is everything. She might ask Pedro if he had a need for a day waitress and he would say, "Sorry, Jacqulyn, all filled up."

Then tomorrow Pedro would say yes, she could fill in and she would tell Pedro that she was sorry as she was engaged with something else. So, this day she took the long walkway to the end of Main Street. She usually stopped short of a long walk because although it was still Main Street and therefore still zoned for businesses, these two or three blocks were mostly residential business orientated like a home with a sign saying seamstress or lawyer. So, as she walked, she took in everything as it wasn't often that she went the whole distance. Her eyes caught a small sign. *Help Wanted*. So, she went to the door and knocked. She explored every option, every time. A chubby dark-complexion lady said yes, and Jacqulyn asked her about the sign. She told Jacqulyn they needed a care keeper for a sick woman, and if she would be interested. Jacqulyn said she would be if the hours were right. So, the woman, whose name was Ingrid, said the hours would be from seven a.m. to four p.m., up to seven days a week. So, Jacqulyn was honest with her and said the hours were fine, and she needed work, but she had no actual experience in caretaking but was willing to learn. Ingrid was impressed with her honesty but in the back of her mind she thought it would never work. Nevertheless, she asked Jacqulyn if she could start tomorrow at seven a.m. and Jacqulyn said yes. That was the reward for taking a walk today.

When she got home, it was about twelve noon and she was starving. Normally, she would have her peanut butter and jelly sandwich and a quartered apple in her purse, but she did not make up anything today as she figured to take a walk and come straight home. Shelly was home reading a book or magazine. She had lunch with Jacqulyn. The conversation started with Shelly saying how much better she liked her new home than the one they moved out of. She especially liked the small yard between the house and a detached car or garage or shed. They never owned a car, so it was a shed. Jacqulyn told her she really liked the house also and that Shelly said she almost forgot to say that someone was interested in renting the bakery store. Jacqulyn thought about it, but she told Shelly that she would pass on renting the space as she wanted to keep her options open. She told Shelly that she might put an office there and she could start her bookkeeping and secretarial service or Shelly might want to do something with it also. So, they both agreed, and the person who inquired was to be told that it was for not for rent right now but things could change. Then Jacqulyn told Shelly that she got a job seven days a week from seven a.m. to four p.m. as a caretaker. Shelly was amazed at Jacqulyn's ability to take any job to save for a rainy-day. They hugged and ate their peanut butter sandwiches while each just ate and spoke a little. It was a very pensive mood. The following day, she went to work for the first time as a caretaker and she was shown her duties by Ingrid, and she was introduced to Constance Anderson who was the person they all took care of. Time flew by kind of rapidly as it always did on a new job as they tried to talk about duties in one long, long sentence. So, it was lunchtime and she sat at the small table, eating her usual lunch. She asked herself if she made the right decision about the rental agreement offer. After all, it probably would have made her and Shelly's life a lot easier. She had no right to assume that her caretaker job was the answer as today's today and tomorrow may not be the same. Constance Anderson was not terribly old but she was sick so that could go on and on or end abruptly.

That first afternoon, Constance asked Jacqulyn to talk to her and get better acquainted with each other. Constance began to say, "I'm an artist and I would rather paint than eat. My parents were exasperated when I painted through lunch or dinner but that's what I love. As you see the living room is filled with paintings, paintings, everywhere. The furniture was delegated to other spaces such as bedrooms. I never appraise the worth of any of my works but apparently, they were good as I was constantly in demand. My parents both died in a boating accident when I was young. So, I lived with my aunt. My parents left me a legacy of bonds and stocks plus the family home. At that time, my aunt was living in New York City in an apartment she could not afford. Her husband was always cheating on her and squandering their money, so they divorced. When my parents probate was over, and I got the title to the home, I asked my aunt if she wanted to come and live in the home with me. She was very familiar with the house as she and her sister really adored each other. She visited often. I did not work, nor did my aunt as we had plenty of money. All I did was paint.

I would drive to the beach — paint the water, the mountains, anything. Sometimes there were sailboats, and I would paint them. I would go to the forest and paint the trees with the sunlight reflecting all different spectrums of color upon the different leaves. I loved it and still do. But my doctors insist for me to stop so I haven't touched a brush now for five years. The minute I saw you this morning the usual came back to me. I said to myself I'd like to paint her. So here we are, we know each other all of five hours and the dormant beast in me wants to kick back the bed covers and paint again. Doctor or no doctor that's what I shall do."

She told Jacqulyn that she got married when she was eighteen years old, but her husband did not want to play second fiddle to a bunch of paint.

"So, he went his way. We were terribly in love, but circumstances prevailed. He joined the Air Force and eventually made Major as a Squadron Leader. He was killed in one of those silly skirmishes in the East. He left me with a lot more money and that was the reward — money instead of love. Now I look back and reminisce and I think I could have given up my passion for painting if I were a little more mature and capable of making adult decisions.

Eventually I opened a small art gallery with a friend, and he was a concierge in art, but he did not paint. He did the selling. He was good. In fact, he comes to see me at least once a month and talks me into letting him sell some of my paintings. We did not especially mesh on the business end because he wanted to go big, and I couldn't care less. So, we dissolved our partnership and sold the gallery which incidentally is still in operation and still doing very well. So, Eric, that's his name, went to New York and opened a grand gallery. I have many photos that I shall show you in time. It was and is a great success and he made a fortune, but his love was not the money. What he savored was selling and appraising. Probably every millionaire or socialite in New York City has some of his recommendations. One eccentric old man has a fireproof vault the size of a small house full of paintings. The amount is estimated to be in the billions. They are not on display but they are there for his personal pleasure. I sympathize with him because it was always hard for me to sell a painting, but I do it for Eric because of our mutual respect. Jacqulyn, let me paint you and I will give you modeling wages besides your caretaker's wages. I would also like to paint your younger sister. Please bring her here."

So in less than eight hours, Jacqulyn had so many offers. Her head was spinning. Constance Anderson was an exceptional lady.

Time went on and she liked her work. She told Ingrid that Constance would like to be in her wheelchair so that she could take her into the garden and paint. Ingrid was all for that as she saw that Constance was just withering away because of the lack of being needed or wanted. So, if she could paint a little it might inspire her again and make her feel like filling a void that should never have been suppressed as her love to paint was greater than life itself. The doctors sometimes were wrong when they thought only of life and death. To Constance, to not paint was death. Sometimes the doctor had wondered if this was the right decision for this person. It was now six months since Jacqulyn started working here. It seemed to her that the workplace did not have many bad positions and that she was lucky, but she now had a taste of several different occupations. The first one was still ongoing after over twelve years. Their newspaper job was three years, but she loved every bit of it so if there had not been that uneventful explosion, chances are, she would have still been there. Shelly was hired as a fill in and she managed to work some weekends for Jacqulyn's and some of Ingrid's time.. . .
. . . Constance thought that Shelly was the ultimate model and as it turned out she was painted many times. Eric visited Constance one time while Jacqulyn was there, and he loved the paintings of Shelly and offered for Shelly to come to New York, and he would see to it that she became a mega star. Shelly declined by saying she had to take care of her sister.. Eric was amazed at how good Constance looked. He saw what she did when she started painting again and remarked that she never lost a thing. He and Constance convened in private sometimes. This one time, he was told that the doctor said she did not have much more time as the cancer was now spreading faster. She confided that Jacqulyn was to get all her

paintings and her photographs plus ten thousand dollars. Ingrid received a substantial sum of money and Eric also received money although he did not need it. Shelly was given five thousand dollars and a letter of recommendation to a prestigious modeling agency. Without the recommendation, one would be whistling Dixie before he got a chance to audition with them. Jacqulyn had a space that she might be encouraged to develop into a painting store — kind of like what we had in our earlier years. *Please help her get started and keep an eye on the progress.*

Constance then died three days later. The probate was read, and it was reported that the rest of her estate went to various charities and artists groups. This did not come about immediately as probates can linger on, but it was consummated within six months. Jacqulyn nor Shelly or Ingrid knew that they were mentioned in the will. A week went by, and she received a letter from the DMV Department that the enclosed pink slip was signed over to her and that the late model Lincoln Continental was hers. All fees had been paid. Jacqulyn also received a letter from Constance's insurance company informing her that she was paid for two years in advance if she wanted to continue working with their company. It was well received and appreciated.

Now she had dollars in the bank, and she was able to save most of what she made working for Constance. Things were looking up for the two sisters, but they never were in the habit of splurging because they never had what it took to splurge. They did live better and enjoyed some of the better things that were offered. About two weeks after Constance's death, Jacqulyn had to endure another bombshell. At this rate she would be an old lady before her time as each one potentially took its toll but so far, she managed to remain untouched. This time it was Mr. Rock who came into the restaurant one evening for dinner. Jacqulyn was so happy to see him that she lost all control and started crying She told Marco's wife to work her shift until she got her composure back. She went to Mr. Rock and apologized for her behavior. Then she went to each table apologizing.

That was why everyone loved Jacquelyn. She always thought of the other person. Mr. Rock had a small steak, green salad, and a large bowl of pasta — no dessert, no wine, only coffee. Between customers, Jacqulyn and Mr. Rock set up an engagement for eight a.m. the next day. He would take her to breakfast, and he had news to tell her. Jacqulyn would ask Shelly to substitute for her tomorrow evening at work. Mr. Rock told Jacqulyn that they had a lot of territory to cover but he was sure that Jacqulyn would probably be back in time to go to work. Mr. Rock arrived at Jacqulyn's property at fifteen to eight a.m., and they left immediately. Mr. Rock took Jacqulyn to a private club that he belonged to. They had a large central dining area plus there were private rooms to hold small meetings. The rooms were air conditioned, and they had a door in the center of each wall facing the central dining area. The rooms were soundproof and had facilities for televisions, computers, andfax machines. To Mr. Rock and Jacqulyn, it was to be used only as a breakfast room but also to discuss the purpose of the meeting. They both ate breakfast in a virtual trance as they were both obsessed with their own thoughts. After a quick breakfast, Mr. Rock began, "My wife is dead. She died from complications from Alzheimer's…"

Jacqulyn gave her condolencesJacqulyn said that before the explosion they were one family then she started to falter and never regained her former self. Mabel's husband passed away and the children had her enrolled in a private nursing home at her request because she did not want to be a burden on her children.

Jacqulyn received a letter from the coroner's office in New Mexico that said they had a body in the morgue with identification of George. He was homeless and incoherent. He walked into the oncoming traffic at a busy street and was killed instantly.

The three chemists from downstairs were now out on bail pending trial. One died a natural death and was discovered by a maid in the hotel he resided in. After two years,the two chemists plea bargained and were sentenced to twenty years each. There were no casualties, or they would have faced murder charges. So that pass was over, and the insurance company had no excuses now to delay payment for Princess Perfume. All were exonerated of all claims by the district attorney's office. So, Jacqulyn's attorney set up a meeting with the insurance lawyers, asking for face value of the policy, plus defamation of character, plus loss of business that was just starting to progress rapidly. For that part, they asked for ten million dollars. They were threatening to sue for twenty-five million dollars. That meant the total came to about fifteen million dollars. The insurance company said they would settle now if they agreed to twelve million five. They would have sixty days to pay the fifteen million dollars if they agreed to that sum. Jacqulyn asked to confer with her lawyer, and it was granted. So, they discussed the counteroffer. She told her lawyer that she wanted two years and could wait another two months to make two million five. So, they went back to the meeting and told the lawyers that they would wait the sixty days for the agreed fifteen million dollars. The lawyers started to pack up when the head lawyer said to write Mr. Rock a check for fifteen million dollars now as he had waited long enough. So, they then went after the district attorney's office.

The head District Attorney at the time that caused all the damage was later relieved of his duties. The new District Attorney did not like the way the former District Attorney tried to bully everyone without an investigation. Jacqulyn was threatening to sue for fifty million dollars for defamation of character with the probable cause of the demise of Princess Perfume. The now District Attorney said he would agree to ten million dollars which they accepted, and the Princess saga was over.

So, since then, Jacqulyn had toyed with the rekindling of the perfume business and starting all over but without Mrs. Rock, she had lost all incentives to do this. Her lawyer received eight million dollars, so she had seventeen million dollars to make another try of it.

I'm sixty-two years old and I really don't need it so I figured we would pay up all we owed and call it quits. So, I figure, that you, Jacqulyn, lost two years of salary plus time was not too good for you so I figured two years of hardship that you endured would be the total of about five thousand dollars, plus I'll throw in another five thousand dollars and if you agree I will give you a check for ten thousand dollars.

Jacqulyn said, "Of course I'll agree. I've never seen ten thousand dollars in any form, even taking care of the books at Princess Perfume."

So, Jacqulyn was relatively rich compared to a few minutes ago. So that part of the business was over. They had to go to the lawyer's office to get him to write her a check. Then Mr. Rock said that he had all the formulas for Princess Perfume in a safe deposit box and if she wanted to make a stab at opening a perfumery that she was welcome to the formulas, and he would have the attorney sign them over to her free and clear. Also, he would be going to Paris soon to invest money into an ongoing perfume business that needed some capital. It was a public company so he would be awarded some shares. He would also be on the board of the directors for the company. He also threw in another protection for her or a potential protection that if she decided to open a perfumery that she could not use Princess Perfume in any form as the name. It now was taboo among the business establishments.

So, they got Jacqulyn's check plus the formulas from the safe deposit box. One thing left to do while they were so close to the cemetery was to put some fresh Flowers on Mrs. Rock's grave as they didn't know when they would be back to the states. They were back at Main Street at about five fifteen p.m. Jacqulyn said that she was tired and that she would let Shelly take her place. They both agreed to pass on dinner so Mr. Rock kissed Jacqulyn on the cheek and they drove off. "Maybe I will see you again and maybe not."

Jacqulyn went home and tried to rest but the day was too emotionally strong and so energy draining. She decided to go to the restaurant and see Shelly and to also grab a bite as she realized that the last food she ate was her breakfast with Mr. Rock. When she got to the restaurant and sat down in an empty booth, she realized that she could not eat anything. What she needed was comfort food as she ordered apple pie a la mode with alarge chocolate milkshake. That did it. After consuming all of that, she still wanted more so she ordered a cup of hot coffee and just sipped coffee and tried to put everything into perspective — all the exhilarating events of the day.

Wow! It was near closing time for the restaurant so she decided to wait for Shelly to end her shift and they could walk home together. When they got home, they slipped into more relaxing clothes and Jacqulyn recapitulated her day. She shook Shelly out of her wits when she was shown the check for ten thousand dollars. Neither of them ever thought they would ever see that much money especially that it was theirs. After scrimping and saving all their life what would they do with ten thousand dollars? Where was all this good fortune leading them into? Was it the proverbial calm before the storm? Was there some substance to the master's scheme?

Jacqulyn had to get out and walk her nervous energy as it was more tiring than working a shift at the restaurant. So, she put on some relaxing clothes, shorts and a white T shirt and sneakers. The day was already starting to heat up so she luckily remembered to put on her visor cap. Shelly was still lingering in bed when Jacqulyn said she was taking a walk and she would bring back some croissants for later. So, she walked up Main Street. Like a magnet she was drawn to the explosion site. She always avoided going that way because of the dread that accompanied the thought and how in a matter of minutes it had wrecked so many lives and dreams. But today, she was going to conquer her fears and never look back. When she got to the site of Mr. Rock's building, she was shocked to see massive trucks and bulldozers clearing the debris. There was a safety guard all around the site as it was a big drop to the basement. On one end of the guardrail was a painted sign with the name of the general contractor and a drawing of what was planned to be rebuilt there. It was a nice three-story commercial building, very modern then there was a realtor sign below the drawing, inviting interested parties to inquire. Apparently, the trauma was over for everyone involved in the explosion and like Mr. Rock, were moving forward. Jacqulyn left the site that was once deemed as her future. She walked here and there with no destination in mind. It was the same old Jacqulyn — never to just walk and enjoy the walk but always observing and looking for an opportunity to make a deal where she could put food on the table.

About 3 St North of Main Street was another street that was generating some interest by investors. The street was different from main as it was not a retail type of environment. The concept here was to remodel the existing building and form an industrial type of landscape to complement their retail extensive Main Street. So, Jacqulyn walked and looked. She came upon a rundown three-story brick building which caught her attention. The sign said *for sale or lease. Please inquire with a name and phone number.* When Jacqulyn went walking, she always wore a belt that had a zipper pack for miscellaneous cans, money — you name it. Jacqulyn unzipped her pouch and removed a small pad and pen and wrote down the name and telephone number. She was quite sure that it was an exercise in futility because she did not believe she would ever call, but something must have stirred in her memory pod as she did take down all the information. She walked about three more blocks on the same street, and she noticed a building that said Sherman's Perfume Company. She was wondering if she recognized the name, but nothing came to mind. As she was searching for her memory back, a heavy-set man with glasses came out of the building. He greeted Jacqulyn and asked her if she wanted to buy. She smiled prettily and said maybe. So, they laughed, and they introduced themselves.

He said, "Come in if you have time and have a cup of coffee and a donut. They are fresh. I realize I left some newspapers in the car so that's where I was going when I saw you. You look very very much like someone that I think I know." He laughed and said, "I guess you think it's the same old con."

Things never change. Jacqulyn and her new acquaintance went into the building. He sat at a desk in a chair that was too small for him, and he told Jacqulyn to help herself to coffee and donuts that were still in their white bag. There was a shelf with some paper cups. She got a cup and poured out some coffee from an automatic coffee maker. While they munched, they talked, and she told him about her start at Princess Perfume and he snapped his fingers and said now that's where he remembered seeing her and again, he laughed. He said to her that he was sorry that he had heard about the explosion. Then a few weeks before the explosion, the day that he allegedly saw Jacqulyn, he said he approached Mr. Rock about buying his perfume business as he was putting all his energy into luxury perfumed soaps. They talked and he asked if Mr. Rock was at all interested but the explosion ended that conversation.

So, he went on to say, "I'm still trying to get out of perfume, but I haven't pushed it. So, I get quite a few people that are interested but for one reason or another it just doesn't work. Twenty thousand dollars and someone gets the whole shebang. Inventory alone is worth over ten thousand dollars. The lab equipment and the tables and the works are all included with the patent and the formulas. What a steal for someone. So, Jacqulyn, do you want to buy? I will sell to you for fifteen thousand dollars, but you must move out of here as I need more room to expand the soap end of it. I can even give you terms. What do you think, Jacqulyn?"

Jacqulyn listened carefully to his offer and gave Mr. Sherman her telephone number and she left. She thought to herself, could she do something with this? On her way home, she remembered telling Shelly that she would bring croissants, so she stopped at a small shop on Main Street that featured croissants and other French pastries. She bought four croissants and two chocolate éclairs filled with whipping cream. They would be dessert for tonight. After buying the fresh bakery items, she hurried home.

Shelly had no place to go but she anxiously awaited her sister or maybe her promised croissant as she put the heat in the oven on. She liked her croissants warm and slathered in butter. If *you're going to indulge, why go halfway it's just as easy to go the full scale.*

Jacqulyn walked in. The two resembled each other. They looked like beautiful twins. They were both the same height, five six or five seven. They both had exquisite body shapes. Jacqulyn might be four or five pounds heavier, and this was attributed to the stress in her life. Shelly was more exuberant and seemed to enjoy each day whereas Jacqulyn was much more reserved. She seldom laughed or joked around. She was all business.

She ran into the kitChan and found a baking pan and popped two croissants in the oven. Shelly put two small plates and a knife and fork by each chair at the table, plus plenty of soft butter, then she asked Jacqulyn if they were still scrimping and where they were on their diet. Jacqulyn was perplexed so she asked what she meant, and Shelly said that she was only heating two croissants. Then Jacqulyn got it and they both started laughing and giggling. Finally, Jacqulyn told Shelly that she could have the other two as she only wanted one, but she did not tell Shelly that she had two glazed donuts earlier. So, they both laughed and again Shelly said that she might just do that — that was, eat the two remaining croissants still in the white bag. So, Jacqulyn removed them from the oven and yelled like a Barker selling peanuts, "Get them all while hot."

SAM CUTRUFELLI SR.

Jacqulyn put another croissant in the oven for Shelly.

"You and I are lucky that our jeans let us eat what we want — in moderation of course — and we don't gain or, for that matter, lose weight."

We were lucky. That evening she went to work preoccupied as she had the perfume dilemma and then out of the blue, she decided to look at the red brick building. *Were the two tied together? Possibly.* Then she got busy with customers and just like that, the conundrum was put on the back burner never to surface again that evening.

She walked home after her shift and then her head started spinning — with Mr. Rock and Mrs. Rock. She had stopped thinking about the Princess fiasco. Sure, it popped in her mind, but never with this consistency. She noticed that Shelly was not home yet, and it was about eleven fifteen p.m. She was generally home at this time unless she had a date. *Calm down, Mother Hen,* Jacqulyn she said to herself. She drank a glass of warm milk hoping that will calm her down, then she noticed a note on her pillow. It was from Shelly. It read : Jacqulyn, I got a call from my friend Mary. We modeled together a few times. She went and broke her leg, so I went to stay with her for a few days. If you need me, you can call this number. I'll call you in the morning and tell you what I know. Have a good night I'll talk to you soon, in the morning at about eight o'clock.

Jacqulyn pedaled around the house for lunch and got hungry for a BLT (bacon, lettuce, and tomato). She liked hers with avocado which she didn't have so she decided to walk to the corner market. It was on Main Street, about a block from her house. The place was always packed because it had the best deli sandwiches which she would normally have but she wanted a BLT. She got her avocado and decided to buy a nice ripe tomato. She found the key to a perfect BLT is the tomato. So, she toasted er bread, put some bacon on top, and she was on her way. She needed extra mayonnaise also, so she started to put together her creation — both slices had mayonnaise on bread then some nice crisp iceberg lettuce, followed by nice thick slices of tomatoes. With the bacon followed a sliced avocado of course salt and pepper — plenty of pepper. She cut the sandwich corners, forming two triangles. If you study geometry, they will have a name for them as they worked perfect triangles; nevertheless, I'm sure perfect triangles or not they would be what the doctor ordered. When she went to the market and opened her purse to pay for the tomatoes and avocados, staring at her on the face was the phone number for the red brick building. *Was this an omen?*

So, after gulping down her BLT and wishing she had made two, she decided to call the realtor. A pleasant voice asked her to hold on a moment. She saidwhat she was calling about was the red brick building on Simmons Street.

She asked Jacqulyn to wait a moment and came back and said that real estate listing belonged to John Bruno, but he was out showing properties. *Can I have your name and phone number and I will have Mr. Bruno call you as soon as possible.*

Jacqulyn excused herself and said she would call back. The rest of the day was uneventful. SHe vacuumed and did the dishes and got ready to go to work.

That night, they were very busy like things are really picking up for Mario and Antonia. The spaghetti was flying out of the kitChan as fast as you could say Jack Robinson. Jacqulyn toyed with the idea of how far the spaghetti would go if all were sold was put into end. What she was going to have for dinner was spaghetti and two meatballs and a green vinegar salad and some French bread. Antonia usually took over her tables while Jacqulyne ate. If she was busy, Jacqulyn ate between customers. Mario had some donuts left from breakfast and he put them in a bag for her. *Mario and Antonio were like my family, and I loved them both.*

In the morning, Jacqulyn awoke with the sun streaming in the window as she forgot to pull the shades down. There was no problem as she naturally woke up at that time give or take a few minutes, but it startled her as she wasn't used to the natural sunlight waking her up. She put on my robe and went to the kitChan to brew some coffee. Mario said to put two donuts in a paper bag and sprinkle a few drops in the bag, not on the donuts. So, she turned on the oven and put two cake donuts plus one plain and one cinnamon sugar in the bag and a few drops of water and popped them into the oven. Presto, the coffee was made the donuts were hot and she enjoyed her breakfast very much. The donuts tasted like they had just come out of the deep fryer, and they were scrumptious.

She relaxed a little, listening to the morning news, when the phone rang. It was Eric from New York. He informed her that the probate had been completed seeing that Constance gave her power of attorney. She was able to have the court give her the envelopes addressed to Jacqulyn and one for her sister Shelly and one for Ingrid. All she had to do was sign for that. There were a few other related parts of the probate that she would discuss with him. She would be flying out of New York tomorrow morning. When she arrived, she would call him.

"Yes, I have your address and yes, I will have transportation as I will rent a car for our week. That's about what I figured it will take to close out everything."

That afternoon, Eric called from the hotel room he rented each time he came to visit. He knew Jacqulyn had to work each evening so he said he would set dinner at the hotel. The hotel had a quality restaurant for its patrons, and it was also available to the public. He told Jacqulyn he would be at her place at eight o'clock a.m. and he would take her to breakfast and to discuss what was happening.

Constance told Eric about the bakery space, but she made it sound like it would probably not be acceptable for an artist shop. She was mistaken as when Jacqulyn saw the space, it was freshly painted and probably two times the size of what Constance and she started with. Jacqulyn did not have the slightest idea of what Constance and Eric were cooking up for her. She would find out shortly.

Eric arrived about seven thirty a.m. and after a welcome kiss and hug, Jacqulyn gave him the grand tour. He was very impressed with the property as it was on Main Street, in the best possible location. The property was probably worth a small fortune and though she sat on a bunch of potential dollars, she still had to scrounge and scratch to make ends meet. Eric thought it was ironic that she hid so much and still really had nothing to help her flight. The money that Constance willed her would help tremendously, of course, and he didn't know about the windfall that she got from Mr. Rock as that just happened a week ago. They got into Eric's rented car to go to breakfast and discuss events. He told Jacqulyn that they would go to a place that was at the very end of Main Street where he and Constance went to for meals when he came to visit her. The farthest Jacqulyn had ever been to was Constance's house.

The restaurant was called Gretchen's Motel and it had about twenty rental units that were very clean and modern. The motel was situated at the end of Main Street and then Main Street turned into Cherry Avenue and went all the way to the next town. The future for all the land around Gretchen's was for a gigantic mall with gaming casinos. If that happened, Gretchen's was right there to capacity. As it was, she was virtually out in the boonies and the only thing that kept her alive was Main Street and the traffic going on Cherry Avenue to the other suburb. So, they drove past Constance's home and about another five miles or so to Gretchen's. Once they passed Constance's property, it was all small farms of one of a kind or the other. One large parcel was a dairy farm and processor of milk. They also made a variety of quality cheeses. So, they went into Gretchen's and Eric was greeted like he was a V.I.P. — very important person. Throughout the dining room, there were paintings by Constance. Eric took Mrs. Gretchen Brinks, the owner, and whispered to her that Constance had passed away. She was shaking as Constance was her friend, as well as a respected customer. Eric asked Gretchen if he could use the banquet room as he had papers to lay out, so she had the waitress prepare a table for them to sit at and some empty tables that he could use for his paperwork. The banquet room was very seldom used as such but occasionally a birthday party or a baby shower took place. Lately, she, Gretchen was having a nice run with weddings.

Eric recommended the 3-egg omelet that both he and Constance usually had for breakfast. That's what Jacqulyn and Eric both ordered. As a special treat and comp of the house, Gretchen served them each a freshly-made croissant with a special milk cheese that was made at the dairy that they passed to Gretchen's. Their breakfast was as good as Eric said it would be and now that Jacqulyn had her car, she and Shelly would probably frequent Gretchen's.

Eric and Jacqulyn moved from the table they had their breakfast at to one of the clean tables that Gretchen said that they could use. Eric opened his briefcase and first thing he did was to hand Jacqulyn her envelope and Shelly's envelope. He had power of attorney and it was his responsibility to get Jacqulyn and Shelly to sign a release. Jacqulyn also signed for Shelly. Jacqulyn opened her envelope and was taken aback. It was a check from Constance for ten thousand dollars. She went from rags to riches in a matter of one week. It was not exactly riches for some people but it sure applied in Jacqulyn's case. She started crying again and it wasn't at all like Jacqulyn, but the emotions just could not be repressed. They were coming at her too fast to block, let alone, analyze. Bang! Here comes another one! Eric told Jacqulyn that they would also include all of Constance's paintings. Constance had paintings scattered everywhere in her house and there were probably at least one hundred to two hundred paintings. Constance painted but very seldom sold her paintings because each one was a part of her. Of course, it helped that she did not need the money. She had all the money she would ever need so she painted and painted. Eric was the only person that she trusted to take some of her paintings to New York and sell them to clients who would respect her art for what it was worth.

Eric told Jacqulyn that to Constance, the paintings were her legacy and incidentally she painted a perfect replica of the front of the bakery. Constance was very impressed instead that she wished she had time to help promote Constance Anderson's studio of art. She tearfully asked Eric and Shelly to help her make her dream a reality. Eric said he would and stated that many studios would not have as many paintings by one famous artist in one location. Without an appraiser, the inventory would be sold and not be replaced with comparable art. Eric met new people that would fill the bill, but if she was available, Melinda Cook would be his first choice. Eric would contact her later that day. Eric said that they had to move fast as the property was sold and the new owners wanted to demolish the house and put a new modern building on the site. It was to be a new car agency. Constance's property was about five acres — all prime property on Main Street. Someone's vision was probably going to be a success. There were many properties on Main Street that met all the requirements for a new car dealership. They had to have the showroom, and plenty of property to display cars on the lot. Constance's property could fulfill all those requirements. Eric suggested that Jacqulyn should rent a space such as an empty store or small warehouse to move the artwork into. He said that if they put everything in the bakery, it could be close. She tried to set up a display. They all agreed, and it popped into Jacqulyn's head that that would include the red brick building. That was located nearby, and she would make a call to John Bruno. Eric called Melissa but she was not in. He left the message and said for her to call him back as soon as possible. Eric told Jacqulyn that Constance and Melissa were very close, and they had lunch or dinner together when it was convenient. Eric started to put his paperwork in his briefcase when Eric had a telephone call. It was Melissa and after their brief exchange of words, Eric said he would like to talk to her about an appraising job. She was all ears, but Eric cut it short and said he would see her today and if she was available, they could go out to dinner. Jacqulyn made an appointment with John Bruno and set it for two-thirty that afternoon, so things were starting to come together.

Eric dropped Jacqulyn to her house and left very quickly. Jacqulyn was surprised to see the Lincoln that was parked outside. She figured that Shelly was probably home. When she went in their house, there was another note saying that her friend was getting along better and that she thought maybe Jacqulyn could use the car, so her friend followed her in her car and stated that she was back at her friend's apartment. That was nice of Shelly, but she was always like that, very accommodating and friendly and never without a kind word or a big smile.

So that afternoon she drove to John Bruno's office. When she walked in the reception room, she announced herself to John's secretary. John's office reception greeted her, and John came storming out. Her first impression was that he was maybe three to four years older, heavyset, about three hundred pounds and overweight., I think maybe he ate too much spaghetti for he was Italian. Instead of a nice formal first time greeting, he came barreling out of his office. Jacqulyn was taken aback by his behavior because two or three people were in the waiting room and they looked up, concerned. One of his associate realtors popped out of his office and noted that it was just John, but he knew that it was John because John was a typical Italian — loud and animated.

John invited her into his office. He closed the door to his office and folded his arms across his chest and said, "Okay, what?"

She was again clueless about this man's behavior. John went on to say, "The other night when I met you and you gave me another name so now you can track me down and now, your name is Jacqulyn?"

He said that he was puzzled. So, he continued, "I went to dinner at my uncle's place and met you." Jacqulyn slammed her head into the palm of her head. She said to him, "Is your uncle named Marco?"

He laughed and said yes, and he said, "Is your name Shelly?"

Now, frown lines were starting to slow on his forehead and beat up respiration were forming. So Jacqulyn continued to say, "I am Jacqulyn and not Shelly and I have worked for your uncle and Antonia since I was 14 years old, 7 days a week or 7 nights, I should say. My sister, Shelly, worked my shift that evening. It's that simple. Shelly is 3 years younger, and they say we could be twins but we're not. Now is everything clear?"

"Yes, yes, clear much, so now so why are you here?"

Jacqulyn was patient and stated that she was interested in the red brick building on Lemons Street and it's just a coincidence about his uncle and Shelly.

"I am going to call the secretary, Pam, so she could pull the paperwork on the Lemons property and get me the keys so we can go look at it."

So, he had Jacqulyn walk out of his office — nothing as dramatic as the entrance that happened. He apologized to her about his transportation because he had to use his brother's dirty pickup.

"It is quite alright. We could go in my car."

When they got to the Lincoln, she handed John the keys and said, "You drive."

This woman is full of surprises. So, he started up and drove to the red brick building. When they got there, he finally got into his comfort spot and started his sales pitch.

"The building was used by a wholesaler. The old man had passed on and the son wanted nothing to do with the building as he was a lawyer in California, and he wanted all the property liquidated and put the building up for sale. There has been little demand for commercial industrial properties, so therefore the building sits."

We went inside and it was a mess — boxes all over the place. John stated that on the roof was a 3-bedroom penthouse where the old man used to live in, so for somebody, it's going to be a very smart move.

Jacqulyn looked past the broken windows and the rubbish and the cobwebs like she was a buyer of real estate all her life. She asked how much the building was. John quoted her a figure but said she could probably get it cheaper — at least $10,000 less. So she said, "Make him an offer reduced by $25,000. I'll come to your office tomorrow to sign the offer and get the paperwork done. I can't do it right now as I must get ready to go to Mario's. Oh, incidentally would you have a small shop or warehouse available for one or 2 months? I just acquired some 200 paintings that I need to store some place."

He said he would inquire around. John drove back to his office and as they were driving, Jacqulyn took out her notepad and wrote the pertinent information for the property offer. *This woman is too much, and I'll be glad to get back to the office and drown myself in coffee. Wow!*

John was so enamored with Jacqulyn that he had to see her again and not later but sooner. So, he decided to go to Jacqulyn's place of work. He sat at a table in her station and said to her that he had located about 4 possible storage sites that she could look at. He also said that he had some paperwork for his uncle to sign. She said to John, "You are so transparent and full of baloney."

All John could do was laugh. He said you can look right through me. The next day, he called the lawyer in California, and he said to him that he had someone interested in the properties. "You finally got a lowball offer."

The lawyer said, "Do what you like regarding the paperwork then send it to me."

When Jacqulyn got home from her work shift, she could sense an anxiety building up in her chest. She was having buyer's remorse. Whatever was she thinking of buying that building or attempting to buy it? Did she think because she had a dollar ahead for the first time in her life that she let it burn a hole in her pocket? Reality would suggest that her plate was full. On the other hand, she could see that the deal for the red brick building was too good to pass up. In one sense, she hoped the lawyer in California would turn down her offer and she would not lose face. She could see that if push came to shove, she could just leave everything, and the deal would pay off handsomely if the economy changed in her favor — all in the hands of a higher power.

The next day was a whirlwind of decision-making. Whatever happened to complacency or just plain old laid back. First, Eric called and said he and Melissa were going to visit the bakery site and plan some moves. "She was very receptive to working with you and she thought that the location was a win-win site."

Eric said she showed her pictures of the inside and out. "Jacqulyn, if we can bag Melissa then we are in the game big time."

Next call was a surprise but not much was surprising Jacqulyn anymore. The perfume man called and was wondering what Jacqulyn thought of his proposal. Jacqulyn did not have time for him right now, so she called and excused herself for not getting back right away to him. She said that she was opening an artist studio at her former bakery property and that she had to deal with moving two hundred or so paintings within ten days. When she would next see him, she could give him more details. He asked for the address of the future studio and said if he were in the neighborhood he would drop by, but he would not impose on her.

The next call was from John Bruno, and she was amazed how that call ruffled her with something brewing, like kind of Cupid and his arrows taking aim? John knew where she lived because he pumped Aunt Antonia so he came over hoping she could have breakfast with him. He also had the handful of temporary storage spaces that he had to show her.

Shelly was still babysitting or nursing her friend, so she was oblivious to the turmoil taking place. Jacqulyn and Shelly usually talked several times a day, but Jacqulyn was reluctant to discuss this chaotic situation over the telephone. So, she asked Shelly if she had time to have dinner at Mario's and maybe if it wasn't too busy, she and Shelly could discuss her current and future. She also stated that she had an envelope for her from Constance — probate that was given to her by Eric.

So, Eric came with Melissa, and they began sizing up the situation. Melissa thought that they needed carpet on the floor as now it was patched-up linoleum. They also thought that Jacqulyn and Shelly would rather have a door cut into the side of the building so that they could enter and leave their quarters without having to go through the studio. Jacqulyn told Melissa and Eric that a friend of hers was a contractor and that she would talk to him. Of course, that friend was John Bruno. She left Erica and Melissa to their own thing as she was just in the way. What they talked about was around how the art would be placed. Eric and Melissa talked about easels in group settings — all stuff that was over her head. Melissa got 2 artists' drawing pads out of Eric's car and they both started measuring and scaling the space so that they could draw in different scenarios. Jacqulyn heard the words easels, pallets in airbrushes, paints. She had to learn how it all worked. She was excited to have Shelly as the assistant of Melissa's as she did not work steadily but was sometimes called for modeling work. She and Melissa thought it could be worked out and of course Jacqulyn was usually available days because she worked nights at Mario's. All in all, it was feasible, and Melissa liked the idea of a live model being in the studio. She saw what Constance saw in Shelly and she was very impressed with her beauty and the natural look that she had. She wanted to meet her assistant as soon as possible.

Just then John Bruno pulled up. He drove a late model car. Jacqulyn introduced John all around and told Eric that she would look at the temporary storage sites. John and Jacqulyn took off. Melissa looked at Eric and said those two showed all the signs of love generating and she laughed. Eric agreed that something was brewing but he was not an expert of such things. For Eric, such events had to mature and finally develop one way or another.

John drove to the bakery of about 2 blocks from Jacqulyn's place and they were going to get some coffee and bakery snacks. They each had coffee and snacks warmed up with some butter melted on the top. John also said he needed the extra calories like he needed a hole in his head. Then John told Jacqulyn about her offer being accepted and that she was making the right choice. Jacqulyn said she would give him his deposit check and he could open escrow. John said that right behind her street was a storefront and a small warehouse in the rear of the store. It was just leased, but the tenant did not have a direct use for the warehouse so he decided to rent it out on a month-to-month basis as his plans might change and he would need the building. He did not want a lease. John said it was relatively cheap and very clean with a concrete drive going to it. John and Jacqulyn finished their coffee, and they went to the warehouse.

The minute Jacqulyn saw it she knew she didn't have to look any further. The building was near her studio which was a plus as they could take their time setting up the studio and not having to drive miles to get some paintings for other necessary items. The place was clean, and it had more than ample storage capacity for their needs. John and Jacqulyn went back to the studio. She told Eric about renting the warehouse and that she could start moving out of Constance's house. Again, Eric was impressed with the vitality of youth. So, John said he would take off from work for a few days and help her move out of the Constance's home and he would rent a large truck and they would begin whenever Eric wanted. Eric had two sets of keys; he gave Jacqulyn one set, and he kept the other. So, he and Melissa would take Eric's car and meet them there. Eric and Melissa went to the deli and bought some ham and cheese sandwiches and chips and sodas for later as they would probably get hungry about lunchtime.

John asked Jacqulyn if she would like to get some samples of carpet to show Eric and Melissa. John said that the owner of the carpet shop was a good customer of his and he knew he could get a great price for Jacqulyn. So, they drove to the carpet shop and got their samples. Then they went to rent the big truck.

Eric and Melissa got to Constance's house and Eric said that they should have a game plan. They decided to start at the back of the house and completely empty one room of whatever they wanted, Then lock the room and move on to another room. John and Jacqulyn arrived, and the truck had a long metal ramp that extended beyond the truck to the ground. Eric and Melissa were to continue moving from back to front and John and Jacqulyn would start loading the truck. They worked feverishly and accomplished much. Eric and Melissa were not as young as John and Jacqulyn, so Eric said, "Let's take a break and eat some lunch." It was any excuse to sit and rest.

The lunch was great, and it was nice for a change to just enjoy each other, eating and talking about nothing. After they ate, John brought the carpet samples to Eric and Melissa, and they agreed the carpet should be a very wearable product. The carpet man said that many of his commercial customers liked a certain color. They picked a certain shade and John got right on the phone and told the carpet man to go to the studio and measure the footage and order it and install it as soon as possible.

John told the carpet man that the key was under the mat by the front door. So, Eric and Melissa continued to move from back to front and John and Jacqulyn continued loading and unloading the truck. Dinner time came around and Eric said he would treat at Gretchen's. It would just be the three of them for John had to drop Jacqulyn off at her house to get ready for work. So, John did just that and went back to Constance's home to load the truck for the last load of this long but exhilarating day.

Jacqulyn's mind was not on serving up spaghetti or pizza, but she kept serving up John, of course in her imagination but it was still yummy. She was quite beat, and Mario noticed it, so it was approaching quitting time and Mario told Antonia to tell Jacqulyn to stop working and to go home and go to bed. Jacqulyn never in her young life heard such sweet words.

When she got home, she noticed the empty truck sitting on the street and young John Bruno was sound asleep in the back seat of his car. She went to John woke him up and said she would make him some coffee, but he knew that one thing could lead to another, so he was being demure and said that he was very tired, but he wanted to make sure she got home safe. It probably was John's hardest decision, but he was not going to push although every nerve in his body said to go. So, he kissed Jacqulyn goodnight and left. Now by this time she was tired, so she said goodnight to Eric and left. Eric drove to his rental unit and that accounted for the studio crew of all four to all be safely in bed because tomorrow would probably be a duplicate of today. Eric thought the way things looked, they could probably wrap it up by tomorrow. So, the next day John showed up at Jacqulyn's with donuts and before he went to the house, he asked Jacqulyn if she had coffee or should he buy her a cup. She said she had a pot brewing and to hurry with the donuts as she was starved.

Eric and Melissa had breakfast at Gretchen's and when they left to go to the studio the truck was already parked, and Jacqulyn and John were sitting in a chair on the porch. They had no keys and regardless it was another excuse for John and Jacqulyn to hold hands and talk. Eric opened and they got right to it. Jacqulyn wrapped each picture in a roll of soft paper that Eric bought at the art store which was used by most studios when they sold a painting. John carefully placed the painting in the truck on the pretense that he would help her wrap paintings. He was now close to her, and they could talk and when no one was looking sneak a kiss or a hug. The truck was loaded and driven to the warehouse and back to Constance's for a repeat performance. Constance had 3 or 4 couches and John put those in first then stacked pictures on the couches. That way the pictures were not making contact with the rough metal floor of the truck. When they exhausted the couches and chairs, they laid the mattress down for the same purpose. It worked out well as Jacqulyn didn't have to wrap the paintings' frames on the bottom. When they got to the warehouse, they laid blankets on the floor and unloaded the paintings. Then the furniture went to another side. Iit was all segregated because Jacqulyn didn't know what furniture she wanted to keep and what she would give to a friend or a charity.

Eric again bought sandwiches and chips and soda for lunch — this time it was Turkey with Swiss cheese. He also bought a loaf of French bread and a pound of roast beef and assorted cheeses for snacks. Constance had a new stainless-steel refrigerator that the lunch meat was now placed in. Melissa said that she would like to have the refrigerator as hers was quite small. Jacqulyn and Shelly could use the washer and dryer as of now. They were never able to save up enough to buy them. They used the local coin laundry mat. Assorted tables and lamps were divided up for whoever wanted what and the rest were brought to the warehouse. There was one more load — a painting plus the load that was ready to go. This was the last load that Jacqulyn would be involved in, and it was time for John to drop her off at home for her night shift, but the others would keep on working until Eric called it a day.

Jacqulyn got to work a little early, so she called Shelly and told Shelly the progress and Shelly griped that she always missed out on all the fun. Fun, hell, it was going to take Jacqulyn a year and a day to recuperate. Next day John proposed to Eric that they could return the big rental truck and John and his brother would finish the moving which consisted mainly of books and removing the free-standing bookcases. So, the move should be all done by today.

Jacqulyn could not work with the moving today as she had previous commitments. Eric and Melissa had some promotional material that had to be approved. It was up to John and his brother to finalize the moving. John was packing books in boxes that his brother picked up for the express purpose to put books in when the superintendent of the contracting firm asked John when the property would be turned over to his team. John told him it appeared as though they would be able to take possession tomorrow, but it was not his place to determine that the super would have to contact Jacqulyn or Eric. He gave this super both of their phone numbers. Jacqulyn was just leaving the house to go to work when John and his brother Paul pulled up and said it was done. They had Melissa's refrigerator strapped to the back rack of the truck.

They made the trip to Melissa's house, but no one was home so their only option was to return to the studio and make other arrangements with Melissa as to when they could deliver the refrigerator. If they couldn't contact her, they would have to put the refrigerator in the warehouse as Paul had a hauling job scheduled for the next day. That was that. Jacqulyn said she had to run and if John and Paul came to the restaurant, she would feed them. It so happened that they could not contact Melissa, so they were forced to put it in the temporary storage and Paul had to leave as he had some more work. John ended up at Maria's by himself and he told

Jacqulyn what they had to do with the refrigerator, and she said it was OK.

The next day was like a breath of fresh air — no pressure, no hectic runs to and from Constance's home. While they were busy moving, John's carpet man put in the carpet. That improvement was worth its weight in gold — the whole studio brightened up. So now it was up to Paul, John's brother to install certain wall sconces and lights above certain paintings. There were also some chandeliers that had to be installed. After that there were some accent paintings of certain walls, and the studio would be ready to be filled. On the outside Paul had to paint the trim around the windows a gold gilt. On each end of the front or two columns that reached to the overhang — Eric wanted those painted in gold. The body of the front was in light gray to accent the gold. After the painting was done the sign painter could put up the sign. It read: Constance Andrew's studio D art. That would be all for Paul regarding the studio, but he still had to cut the doorway in the side of the building so Jacqulyn and Shelly could be separated from the studio. A three-foot brisk walkway had to be put in because presently it was a small side yard with grass. Paul was a hard worker and knew the trades well. He also had two helpers who were proficient with their tasks so it would not take long. Melissa and Jacqulyn could open shop. Eric told Jacqulyn that he would foot the bill for all of Jacqulyn's expenses to date.

John did not want any money. He told Eric to write a check so that the studio would have a starting bank in the cash registers. Paul and Melissa received generous checks. Melissa welcomed her check because she had not worked for over two years. The place she worked at for many years — the owner decided to call it a day and retired the shop and Melissa ended up without a job. Most everywhere that she went to apply for jobs she was told the same thing: that they all had theerir own art appraisers in line. Melissa was never so happy as when she met with Eric and the job was offered to her. Jacqulyn and Melissa hit it off well and they really respected each other. They kept plugging away so that progress was evident every day. The perfume man kept calling Jacqulyn and she told him that she had to put him on the back burner because she was committed to a timetable to vacate Constance's home. As soon as they were done, she would contact him. That was the best she could see under the circumstances. In the meantime, the escrow was closed on the red brick building. It was not priority number one today so it would have to sit as it had been for one and a half years until she could devote some time to it. It was a luxury that she had no time for, but it was always in the back of her mind. Shelly finally got to the point that her friend was mobile and could get along slowly but surely but without her help now. Shelly came home and was ever so glad to be home. Jacqulyn and Shelly had a lot of catching up to do and of course Shelly and Jacqulyn talked each day, but it was not the same as physically seeing the transformations to the bakery or physically seeing and going into the red brick building.

Shelly finally met Melissa and she was so anxious to get to work that she almost forgot she had to model at a department store the next day. After that, her calendar was clear until she got another gig so she was looking forward to the day after tomorrow so she and Melissa could work together. Oh, incidentally Constance gave Shelly a check for five thousand dollars from her probate and in a separate note, she thanked Shelly for modeling for her. Shelly was paid handsomely for the modeling, so the five thousand dollars was just a way of saying thank you.

Eric suggested that Melissa put some small ads in the different local newspapers announcing the opening of Constance's studio soon. Melissa an old-time appraiser would be the appraiser and the studio manager. She would like for all people interested in art to come in and introduce themselves. Of course most painters knew Melissa as an appraiser for some of the largest auction houses and art studios. Melissa said that the new studio would have over two hundred paintings that the famous artist had painted. *We welcome all painters to bring in their artwork and let Melissa appraise them. We will also have selected artists hold shows with their paintings and to contact Melissa if you have any interest to display your art.* The studio also had a famous local model working with Melissa. She was available to model for interested painters. *So long for now although we're not officially open, drop by and say hello.* Melissa and Shelly composed something and with the help of an advertising expert they were able to produce a unique ad. The ad was a huge success and it brought in numbers of painters and interesting people. Of course, many were just curiosity seekers but all in all the ads were a huge success. Melissa was ever so grateful for Shelly's help as Melissa was so busy promoting and managing with the people that sometimes she thought if Shelly were not there to continue setting up displays,the setting would come to a complete halt. Shelly had to go to the warehouse and bring back a load of paintings, to clean and dust them and arrange them as Melissa had described. Shelly was a fast learner and soon her eyes told her work groupings a painting belonged to. Jacqulyn was not idle at all. She just was not part of the setting up, but she did run all the errands and made purchases like art materials. She also bought a cash register and acquired pieces of furniture for the studio.

Melissa had thought that in about another two weeks they would be ready to open. Eric was not around, and he had to go back to New York where his famous art studio was located. He liked to think that it was imperative that he did not stay away too long. His studio in New York was probably there five or ten years so I imagine it could exist for a week or so without its owner. Eric's studio was busy, and he constantly spoke of Constance's studios and about Melissa being there and he talked about the two-hundred or so pieces of art painted by Constance that were there. There were also the two or three photographs of paintings by Constance's other famous artists. So, he encouraged painters and buyers to visit Constance's studio if not to buy or sell paintings then just to browse through the hundreds of Constance's. Eric was scheduled to go back to Constance's studio for three days. This time he elected to be closer so when the time came, he would be reserving a unit at GretChan's.

Mister Perfume Man and Jacqulyn finally met to talk about the sale of his perfume business. The last time they talked he told Jacqulyn that she could have the whole business for ten thousand dollars. Jacqulyn asked the perfume man for a dozen or so bottles of his perfumes so that she could try to get a feeling for his products before she made any decisions.

So, she arrived home with about twelve bottles and told Shelly about them and what she thought about them. She could not stay long as she was to be at work within the next half an hour. Every perfume person knows that if you do not have a nose for perfume, you really are handicapped. Shelly was not a perfume smeller. She had the nose for it as she could smell and eliminate and this certain one had possibilities. The perfumer's nose was not learned; it was a gift you had, or you didn't have. Shelly got a few bottles of her own perfume, some of Jacqulyn's, plus the perfume man's and she started smelling and making notes. Her conclusion was that the perfumes were worthless for women, but with certain additions it could possibly be an absolute product for men's deodorant. Men's deodorants and senses were not nearlyas big as women's, but it was just beginning to take off.

She called Jacqulyn at work because she was so very excited, and she briefly told Jacqulyn what she discovered. She said that she should hurry home so she could demonstrate, and she also asked her to bring her a piece of apple pie as she was starving — this stress was causing her to require something sweet. *We have ice cream so just bring on the pie.* Jacqulyn was excited because she knew Shelly had premonitions. Jacqulyn remembered when Shelly was ten or eleven years old her school was having a catered buffet. The principal who happened to be Shelly's teacher asked for some of the favorite students to help with seating and putting place cards for the guests. So, the caterers brought in the food and Shelly helped unload the catering trucks when suddenly Shelly stopped in her tracks. Something was wrong with one of the entrees. She told the principal and the caterer was listening. Shelly explained that there was something wrong with their dish. Well, the caterer lost his cool and told the principal that little so and so was a brat and to get her out of here or he was going to pack up and leave.

"Mother prima donna," said the principal to herself so she politely told Shelly that she appreciated her help, but she could now go home as the catered would take over. The next day the headlines were screaming that twenty or so people at the principal's gathering became ill with food poisoning. The main speaker guest was so ill that they thought that she would not make it. She was moved into intensive care for one week before they finally got a handle on it, but they could not come up with any previous poisonings of that magnitude or even diagnosed what it was. The school was sued by some of the hospitalized people, but everything was hushed up and the school board paid out many hundreds of dollars. Shelly was interrogated and they just thought she had said something that came to a child's head, but they never gave Shelly a chance to show her powers for it not to be be exposed as an I-told-you-so incident.

Many times after that, Shelly proved that she was far above average when it came to taste and smell. If animals could talk, they would be able to tell people a lot about taste and smell as animals throughout the world were used to sniffing out illicit drugs, smelling a convict's clothing and pinning him down in some attic or basement.

So, Jacqulyn brought the pie and Shelly had a pot of coffee brewing. They were going to feast before Shelly's demonstration. There was nothing like apple pie a la mode at any time, but it is especially good after watching a good movie and before going to bed. So, Shelly began her demonstration as best she could. After all, she was not a chemist but relied solely on her image ability to separate smells. Shelly told Jacqulyn that by adding some of her perfumes to the other perfumes it made a distinct odor that would appeal to men and with the aid of a master chemist it could probably become a male deodorant. She was close enough to figuring it out, but she didn't have the hundreds of sample smells that it would take to perfect the men's deodorant and to have longevity to the product. So, Jacquelyn said she would write to Mr. Rock and explain Shelly's discovery and thoughts.

It so happened that the company that Mr. Rock invested in sold out to a big conglomerate and they had many talented chemists on their board, so they agreed to give Mr. Rock and other board members of the bought-out company. Severance pay plus shares in the company were given. Mr. Rock decided to just take all cash and end his romance with investing and living outside of the U.S. He now had so much money that he lamented: *if only I had youth and ambition to go with it,* but wishful thinking was not reality so he had to live the rest of his life as so many multi- millionaires did — playing politics or if they were physically able, indulging in golf. But one thing was for sure. He would let the players play the investing game. When you had millions, why would you need more millions?

There were pros and cons to that kind of thinking — better let it rest. Anyway, he wrote back to Jacqulyn that he would be coming home soon but soon could be six months to a year or more because these large corporations moved as fast as a snail then there were tax problems to be addressed. If he did not settle his affairs completely, he would get them started and possibly come home for a bit and travel back and forth as was necessary. Jacqulyn and Shelly were a little disappointed but they could do little and they did not have the experience and know-how to hire a strong chemist so they figured that the enthusiasm would have to be curbed until Mr. Rock came home.

Jacqulyn made up her mind that she would not try to offer perfume man any amount of money because as a perfume the product was worthless. That's why it was a failure in the essence market. It might be worth something as a base for some other product such as Shelly suggested. If the product wasn't saleable then it was not for Jacqulyn as she nor Shelly were chemists, but if the product was sellable than they could produce it and market it. So, for the time being, , Redbrick building would have to sit.

Constance Anderson Studio de Art was very close to being opened. The professional assessment was very favorable. Artists and potential buyers were coming from all directions to appraise the studio. There weren't many studios in the U.S. that had such an extensive amount of live art from such a distinguished artist. Constance knew that afer her death, her legacy would be fulfilled by Eric, Melissa, Shelly, and Jacqulyn. Eric was the force that would never let go of a commitment and she had a commitment to Constance. When he arrived at the studio, he was overwhelmed at the result. Eric started and sold many studios in his lifetime, but this was probably the most promising of the lot. A few dedicated hard-working people and an artist extraordinaire turned the ugly duckling bakery into a graceful white swan.

The opening was very successful and now five days later it was still amazingly busy. It seemed like buyers were waiting to see and buy Constance's enormous collection. The buyers were surprised because Constance did not put her work up for sale so when the studio opened the starved buyers were more than eager to open their wallets. It was beginning to look like what Eric feared — that the inventory could be depleted faster than it could be replaced. But the artist was starting to sell their work to Melissa because of the confidence they had in her. She could make an artist famous if they had the talent. So, shows were being held and whatever it took to promote a perspective artist was done. Art was just a word but put it on canvas and it could be worth millions of dollars as many paintings were. Before Eric came back to Constance's studio, he selected 50 or so paintings that he thought were good to help replace inventory. Eric had a special code that Melissa and Shelly could decipher and so when they sold a painting, they always looked for Eric's code so that he would be paid for his paintings. In other words he put a small fortune on consignment to the studio. *Could you imagine $300,000 worth of paintings at your disposal, and you didn't have to mortgage the farm to have them?* Not only that, but after a certain amount of Eric's inventory was sold, he would send over more so the studio always looked jam-packed and Eric only sent top artists' work so Melissa and Shelly could advertise that they have art from any number of prestigious painters. A

Melissa was a gifted appraiser. She had a knack or sense of what had to be, how to make an art studio click. First and foremost, everything had to be of professional quality. Brushes, frames, artist colors — whatever went into the studio was prime quality. Melissa was able to open different segments to make a whole, the same way a grocery store would feature its meat and fish and have a vegetable department or bakery department to make a complete grocery store. Melissa's concept was similar. She added a complete section or department that sold artist colors and tints, artist brushes, canvases, art paper, lacquers, easels. Each item was professional. She next developed a picture frame department along with the shop to make custom picture frames but she soon discovered that they lack the space for that. So, that department was moved to the warehouse on Sherman Ave which was only a block away in the street over from Main Street. To promote the picture frame department, Melissa had some representative frames for customers to see and samples of wood and types of coloring. A sign also let people know that they had a complete stock of frames at their warehouse location. Melissa never seemed to be amazed at the beauty that was Shelly. Not only did she become indispensable in a very short time, but the modeling was the department that was fast becoming a big money machine. Artists were frantic to arrange time for Shelly to model — either just the face or the whole body. It got to a point where Melissa had to bring in models to satisfy the artists. One of the more in-demand models was Shelly's friend who was in the skiing accident. She was all healed up and beautiful and she was almost a permanent part of the studio, but she was only by appointment. *Charge their customers fees and give the studio their commission.* It seemed to work out perfectly for all concerned. Smaller department stores and agencies were starting to come to the studio when they were overloaded or when they did not have a model in attendance.

As the studios entertained such success Jacqulyn and John were not quiet on their front. It turns out that Mario and Antonio were closing the restaurant tomorrow for a two-week vacation. It was a blessing for Jacqulyn as she worked in the studio and still waitressed in the evening 7 days a week. Only youth and perseverance could keep up with that pace for any length of time, so this evening was going to be a sigh of relief for it was to be the last work evening for all in the restaurant for 2 whole weeks. The shift was rapidly coming to an end when John called and told Jacqulyn that he was starved and asked Antonio to save him a big plate of pasta and 2 meatballs. Jacqulyn did not have supper yet as she was waiting for John. John got there in about 10 minutes. They were going to eat in the kitchen so that it did not appear to other customers that the restaurant was open becausethere was a closed sign hanging from a nail on the door.

So, while John was eating, he was also planning. Jacqulyn was soon to find out. John had a mouthful of spaghetti when he put it out to Jacqulyn that he would like to marry her now. Jacqulyn was startled but came to her senses fast. She told John that the most ardent devotees to the art of proposing marriage usually got on their knees and held the lady's hand and ask for her consent. John just looked at her as if to say that he was so much in love that he did not have time for such formalities. Also, he was eating. So, Jacqulyn took a big mouthful of spaghetti in her mouth and she said yes, sending a spray of tomato sauce and spaghetti John's way. But all John was aware of was that one word, yes. So, without further ado he told her to pack some things and they would leave right now for Reno and tie the knot. John already had his suitcase packed. He was so confident and prepared for the best outcome. Jacqulyn ran home, packed a bag and left a note for Shelly withouttelling her what John and Jacqulyn were contemplating. She said they would call her in the morning.

The wheels of fortune changed again. Mario and Antonio left for their vacation. Jacqulyn and Shelly gave them $10,000 to enjoy their time off. The wheel went around again with Mario and Antonio helping Jacqulyn and Shelly live. Mario had givenJacqulyn his wages since he was 14 years old and still going to school. She was 11. It was hard to imagine that 2 girls aged 11 and 14 faced the world as grownups. So now Shelly had gotten a substantial amount of luck and fortune. Jacqulyn and Shelly also gave Hans the cook $1000 so he could have a little vacation. Hans was German, all of 6-foot 3 and about 250 pounds. When he was 17 years old, he asked Mario for a job. Hans Schultz did not like school, so he decided to leave school and be a cook. His father was German, and his mother was Italian. German food was almost never on the table at the Schultz 's mainly because Han's mother did not know the first thing about how to prepare it. Han's mother made the best spaghetti and meatballs ever. She also made scrumptuous lasagna. Hans was taught very early the secrets of Mrs. Schultz's specialties. So, when Hans went to work for Mario, he told him that he cooked a mean spaghetti with meatballs and lasagna. Mario was very impressed mostly because before Hans came, he had to do it all and Hans could take some of the burden off his shoulders. Mario's Italian restaurant was not a household name. They struggled and scrimped like most mom-and-pop businesses. Hans, at age 17, helped turn Mario's fortune around. True to his word Hans' spaghetti and meatballs was a hit. He was dubbed Hans the German Spaghetti Man. People came from all over to share Hans' and Mario's spaghetti. Mario did his share by not stretching on the meal and supplied garlic for the bread. Mario said the spaghetti was cheap so they gave the customers a good portion. It also paid off handsomely as people knew when they went to Mario's they got their money's worth. Another specialty at Mario's was the minestrone soup that Antonio made. It was served 7 days a week and it was good especially with homemade garlic bread that Mario made. So, Jacqulyn and Shelly felt good that they were able to reciprocate and help these 3 people who help them so much. Hans treated Jacqulyn as an equal, so Jacqulyn never lost her composure. She was a breadwinner at 14 and didn't want anyone to forget it.

For 7 days and nights all John and Jacqulyn did was gamble and eat a lot and of course make love a lot. After 7 days of loafing the newlyweds came home and plunged right into their duties as if they had never left. The only difference was that Jacqulyn did not have to work in the restaurant for another week. Mr. Rock arrived in the United States and upon arriving called the studio and asked for Jacqulyn. Melissa answered the phone and told Mr. Rock that Jacqulyn was not available, and she identified herself to him. Mr. Rock identified himself to Melissa and she was ecstatic. She told Mr. Rock that she had been hearing of him for months. He said that he was going to rent a car and then register into a hotel. Melissa suggested that he called Gretchen and set up a unit as it would be more convenient than driving all the way to and from the airport. Gretchen was just down the street from the studio. Melissa got Gretchen's phone number and she gave it to Mr. Rock. She also suggested that if Mr. Rock wanted, she could make the arrangement with Gretchen. Mr. Rock thanked her and said he would call Gretchen.

The next morning Mr. Rock was at the studio before it opened. Melissa pulled up a few minutes later. They introduced themselves and Melissa said she would run down to the bakery and get some coffee and croissants. This pleased Mr. Rock as he was used to having a continental breakfast during his stay in Paris. With the goodies, they went into the studio and sat at a small table to sip coffee and eat croissants. It was still early as the studio didn't open until 9:00 am so Melissa gave Mr. Rock a tour of the place. Mr. Rock was very impressed because the last time he saw the former bakery, it was an ugly duckling. Melissa called Shelly and told her Mr. Rock was there. Shelly asked to speak to him, so Melissa handed Mr. Rock the telephone and said it was Shelly. They had a nice conversation and Shelly said she was just leaving the house. She would see Mr. Rock in a few minutes.

Shelly and Mr. Rock embraced like a father and daughter rekindling from a long-time separation. They sat down and had coffee. Melissa got up and said it was time to open the studio. She told Shelly and Mr. Rock to continue their coffee as she would greet the customers. There were about 3 customers waiting to enter and two of them seemed to know where they wanted to look. The 3rd customer hesitated close to the customers' ring out table. Melissa was there and she talked to the customer and invited her to Constance's studio. Melissa offered her a cup of coffee which she declined but was thankful anyway. Then she introduced herself and handed Melissa a business card. She said her name was Priscilla Chan and she represented her father, Mr. Oh Chan of Oh Chan industries. "It appears that one of Mrs. Chan's father's executives happened to be in the area when you opened the studio. He knew of what my father's taste was in art as he has an extensive collection. Incidentally my father's broker is Eric Mueller who has the art studio in New York. Eric and my father were at a banquet for artists and Eric told my father that Constance passed on but that the studio that planned to open represented a large portion of her legacy and that Eric was actively overseeing the project. So, my father's executive who also deals in art and deals with Mr. Mueller wasn't exactly just in the area, but my father asked him to appraise the studio. He reported back to my father that it was well stocked with Constance's work, but also other artists and it would behoove him to visit the studio. He also said there was a portrait of a model that appeared interesting, and he wrote down the code number. He also took some photographs to show my father."

It so happened that the portrait was the girl model that Shelly was caring for during her convalescence. Mr. Chan had a liking for head portraits as he said that an artist's worth was how he accented the eyes as they expressed the innermost feelings of the model. If the artist was gifted enough, the eyes told a lot of stories, imagined or not. Mr. Chan liked to look into the eyes of the still life and see his own version of what those eyes represented.

Melissa looked up the code and sought out the painting. The painting was done by a very gifted artist that shot the photo of Shelly and asked Melissa if she could reserve a spot for him so he could paint her. The price was $3000.00 and Melissa and Miss Chan both agreed that it was reasonable. The painting wasto be packed and shipped to Mr. Chan's office. Miss Chan gave Melissa the address and left.

Melissa knew that Shelly would be really pleased that the portrait was sold. Kelly made her family money but if the artist was generous he would give her an additional bonus. That way, the chemistry between the model and artist was further enhanced. She was happy to tell Mr. Rock of her and Kelly's modeling together, even before the studio was opened. Mr. Rock had no plans, so he just hung out in the studio. Customers who came in and out were all treated as family as Jacqulyn insisted that no one was to be overlooked because a browser today might be a buyer tomorrow. So that was to be Jacqulyn's promise. *You come to conferences as equals and leave as friends.*

Lunchtime was divided between Shelly and Melissa so one of the two were usually always on hand. Melissa said she would take Mr. Rock to lunch. Mario's was closed, so Melissa took Mr. Rock to Gretchen's for lunch. They both ordered their preference and found that they enjoyed each other. Melissa called Shelly and asked if it was busy and if not, she and Mr. Rock would linger over coffee and dessert for an extra 15 to 20 minutes. Shelly said that she and the new salesperson could handle it and for Melissa and Mr. Rock to stay out if they wanted. Shelly told Melissa that she would call her if he needed to. Mr. Rock was smitten with Melissa and vice-versa, but they both knew their priorities and so Mr. Rock paid the bill and they left Gretchen's to return to the studio.

Shelly and Amy started to feel some hunger pains, so she gave them some money and told her to go get some deli sandwiches and soft drinks. They ate mouthfuls between customers, and it worked out fine. Amy was a freshman art student who had to work and go to college, so she was grateful to Melissa and Shelly. Normally Amy went to school until 2:30 pm but today she had the day off from school and that was the reason she was there for lunch and was working today. She also worked full time on Saturdays and Sundays. Amy was really pleased with herself as she made a big sale to a young man. He was sponsoring his girlfriend who wanted to be an artist. So, Amy told them that she was an art student and that broke the ice. So whatever Amy suggested was paramount for her success. The young couple bought easels, pads, paint and charcoal and asked if they could pick her brains and get advice from her from time to time. Amy said she would be happy to advise her. The studio would help her as Shelly was a model and Melissa was an appraiser. It was just in time for Mr. Rock to talk to Jacqulyn as they were going to leave Reno that evening and she would see him. So, Jacqulyn talked to Melissa and Shelly and hung up.

Mr. Chan called Eric and they said their hellos. Mr. Chan got right to the point. He asked Eric if he had any head portraits that

Constance painted, and Eric said he had two heads and four full body portraits of the same girl. He told Mr. Chan outright that they were not his, that they belonged to Constance's legacy, but he could get it here in New York on consignment. "I was interested to not sell them to a dealer but to a collector. I could send them to your office, or I can put them aside for you to see at your convenience."

Mr. Chan said that he would be there tomorrow at 2:00 pm. He apologized to Eric as he knew that not everyone saw what he wanted to see. He told Eric he was looking for more depth — it could be sorrow or happiness he didn't quite know but if he saw something, he would recognize it.

He went on, "In my collection I must have 40 head portraits. You sold me quite a few. They are good or I would not have bought them. Not tell an artist or for that matter an appraiser like yourself what you want to see. An appraiser will show you a painting that is excellent and worth millions but rejected by some because of what they didn't see. Do you understand? But my days of just buying art are gone, now I want to see death, so I don't feel remorse if I do not buy it. I have plenty of years left in me that I don't have to rush just to buy. That being said, I will see you tomorrow. Besides Constance's paintings, I will look around. I'm not so naive that what I want is the only thing I'll keep on buying but in a different plateau."

The next day Mr. and Mrs. Bruno came into the studio. It appeared to Melissa that they appeared kind of sheepish, maybe it was because the love bug caught them, and they didn't have a whirlwind affair. What happened to John and Jacqulyn came directly from the heart. No, it does not mean that one way is better than another. It just means they're different. Yes, love can be earned or learned but usually it's because of a different catalyst. It might be longevity. In might be consideration one has for the other. It could be security — children put in. It really is not called love. They are always there for each other. Someone you know is there. No one can replace the other but it's steady and for the outsider, it might be said that they are the ideal couple. The other might be more spontaneous. They might end up the same as the longevity type, but they just seem like every day is honey.

John and Jacqulyn were back, and Shelly was beaming. Mr. Rock had not had a stir in his body for a long time. They were all happy for each other. Even the customers were caught up in the happiness. They would probably leave the studio and tell someone over dinner what a delightful day she or he had.

In New York, Eric was about to show Mr. Chan the paintings of Shelly that Constance painted. Eric was a professional, so he knew not to push. He casually put one on an easel and repeated, "So all six paintings by Constance's are on easels."

Eric made sure that the lighting was right, and he excused himself and left Mr. Chan to himself. After an appropriate amount of time Eric came back to the area that Mr. Chan was. It was kind of like deliberate on a verdict. The lawyers always tried to determine their verdict by the juror's demeanor. Were they jubilant? Eric was doing the same, as if he saw a smile or a point on Mr. Chan's face, he would assume something, but he was not always right. Mr. Chan said, "I'll take all six and send me the bill and Eric, I congratulate you on being so perceptive that you knew exactly what I wanted. You're a good friend."

Mr. Chan did not ask for the price as it did not mean anything to him. It was the exhilarating feeling that here was life, here was what other painters could not see although they might all be painting the same model. Constance was one of a kind and in his lifetime there probably would not be another Constance. If we were talking money, the six paintings would put Constance's studio in the black for many years to come. Eric knew that Mr. Chan would never sell Constance's paintings because he was a man of his word. No contract was needed. *I'm sure in his will he would specify that the paintings were never to be sold again.* Eric had tears in his eyes not because of the fortune but because of his love for Constance and Jacqulyn and Shelly. His love for Constance was about as great as a love can be for thirty or so. They never had an affair but the mutual love for each other was boundless. His love for Jacqulyn and Shelly was not unlike a father's love for his daughters. He considered himself fortunate that this experience was his experience.

He immediately called the studio. Melissa answered and he told her about the fortune that befell upon them. Shelly was there but was busy with a customer. John and Jacqulyn left. Amy left also. It was Mr. Rock and Melissa who were free to talk to Eric. Eric said that he would be going to California for an art show and would come early so that he could spend some time with them. Jacqulyn always treated everyone as equals and now the gods were reimbursing her. So, he was so glad that he lost his perspective and hugged and kissed Melissa. Yes, it was Cupid on the prowl. Mr. Rock got a hold of himself as quickly as he lost it. He stepped out on the street and lit up his pipe. Shelly finished with her customer and came over to Melissa and asked what that demonstration was all about. Melissa told her that Eric called in to say all six of his paintings from Constance sold for a small fortune. She should faint or cry. She did neither. She just pulled up a chair and looked out into space. "If you're patient enough and don't let anyone crowd you into a corner and batter you to death, you do have a chance to see things turn sometimes ever so slow, but the gears are clicking."

Shelly and Melissa prepared to close. It was approaching seven p.m. and that was closing time. Today was a long exhilarating day. Eric recommended that they have a burglar alarm installed which they did. But Shelly was too anxious to set it properly, so she asked Melissa to do it. They took turns after five-thirty to seven p.m. so that they each got off a few hours early but tonight she was glad that Melissa was still here as she and Mr. Rock were in the backroom talking. So, Melissa set up the alarm. She was doing everything right except she did not punch in the accepted button, so the alarm didn't engage. After three tries, the alarm would automatically stop functioning until a new set of passwords were incorporated into the system. So, Shelly used up two chances and didn't want to cope with messing up the 3rd time so she asked Melissa to do it. If Melissa didn't happen to be there, she would have had the hassle of waiting for a serviceman from the alarm company. She thanked Melissa and told her and Mr. Rock that she would see them both in the morning.

Melissa and Mr. Rock were sitting in Mr. Rock's car. It was dinnertime and Mr. Rock said they should eat together. Thankfully it was what Melissa hoped she would hear. They both agreed that they did not want to go to Gretchen's especially because they thought too many eyes would be upon them. After the eyes, the mouth might start working. So, they decided on a southern style chicken dinner with all the trimmings — mashed potatoes gravy and corn.

After dinner, Mr. Rock drove her to her car but Melissa asked, "Would you mind taking me home and tucking me in?"

"It would be my pleasure, Melissa."

So, a precedent had been set without either of them realizing it because that was to be Melissa's last time to come home without Mr. Rock.

It was so hard to believe in less than a year Jacqulyn and Shelly became millionaires. Most of the bounty was in real estate and inventory but they could now afford to spend reasonably or buy whatever they wanted. The keyword was reasonably, but Jacqulyn and Shelly never had much, so it was easy not to get carried away and mortgage themselves to the limit. Jacqulyn had the Lincoln. Shelly might or might not want a new car.

The next day, after everyone got settled in. Breakfast was over and this studio was open. It was Mr. Rock's time to step up and praise

Shelly's feelings about the male deodorant. Mr. Rock said he would need a Bunsen burner and a table and assorted chemicals. He said that he could use a burner that had a hose to a tank for the time being. Today was Saturday so the studio would have a full crew, but Jacqulyn and Shelly would be mostly involved with Mr. Rock at the warehouse behind Main Street. Once Shelly reveals to Mr. Rock what she discovered by smelling then Shelly would go back to work at the studio. So, Shelly began detailing her newfound theory. Mr. Rock was very attentive. When Mr. Rock was in charge, there was no room for error. He was strictly business. Nice cities were not Mr. Rock's forte. When he was at the helm and if someone was doing well, he would be the first to congratulate him or her.

She got out a fresh bottle of perfume — a man's perfume — and told Mr. Rock what she added to the base to obtain what she thought could be made into a male deodorant. Shelly let Mr. Rock smell the product that she and Jacqulyn produced. Mr. Rock was impressed. Mr. Rock now had the direction Shelly was going into. Being a chemist did not necessarily mean one had the nose or smell that someone like Shelly had. But they could carry the smell into something more tangible by adding force — stop stick shooting different chemicals. It's a trial-and-error thing. The nose always must be there to reject or approve the experiment. So, Shelly would be running back and forth from the warehouse to the studio. Saturdays, Amy would be there all day with Melissa. Amy was not a very experienced artist or salesperson, but she wanted to learn so she was very willing to take whatever comes along. She always had Melissa there to answer any questions that might come up. Amy was not just a body. She was a star in the making, both as an artist and a retail clerk. If she diligently followed up on both, she would become an appraiser as well. Most appraisers would learn from the endless souls they made because each artwork had its own peculiar properties. Soon, a person could look at a painting and say this is so-and-so's style and therefore make a stab at pricing the art. It did not come overnight, and it did not necessarily come to everyone, but some had the capacity to even out and Amy was one of them.

Back at the warehouse Mr. Rock told Jacqulyn that Shelly was on the right track and if they could come up with a saleable product, it could be a blockbuster as the male deodorant incense business is about to come into its own. So, the first runners were always going to be ahead of the pack. So, Mr. Rock said that he needed some chemicals that they didn't have, and he asked Jacqulyn to make a run and try to get them. Ordinarily there was a wholesale company that was just blocks from the old Princess Perfume shop, but it was not open on Saturdays and Sundays. Mr. Rock remembered that the owner liked to go in on Saturdays and catch up on loose ends. Mr. Rock and the owner were very good friends and Mr. Rock was a very appreciated customer, so Mr. Rock called the chemical company. Usually the old man didn't answer the phone when he was there. But this time he did and to his surprise it was Mr. Rock. So, Mr. Rock gave him a rundown of events since the explosion and said he just got in from Paris and was thinking of getting back in the saddle. So, he was experimenting with some formulas and hopefully hit upon something. He needed a few chemicals for his experiment, and would it be OK for him to send Jacqulyn. The old man knew Jacqulyn from Princess Perfume and he always kidded Jacqulyn that he would give a fortune to be young as her. "Oh, Jacqulyn, we could make such beautiful music together if I was 50 years younger."

Something like that always transpired with the old man in Jacqulyn. So, he told Mr. Rock to call his order in and he would pack it and give it to Jacqulyn. Being a businessman first, he asked Mr. Rock if he should open the book for him and under what name. Mr. Rock said it was premature but to open the account as Mr. Rock and gave a temporary address — the warehouse on Sherman Ave. As soon as he had time, he would be over to see him, and they hung up. True to his word, he had the order ready for Jacqulyn. He looked much older in two or three short years but that's to be expected. He was close to a young eighty years old. Jacqulyn brought Mr. Rock the needed chemicals. Just as Jacqulyn got settled, she received a telephone call from the perfume company. It was imperative they meet so Jacqulyn set up a three-p.m. appointment. She told Mr. Rock what was happening. She thought that perfume man was at a point that if something didn't happen between him and Jacqulyn, he would probably liquidate the business piece by piece. Jacqulyn told Mr. Rock about the twenty-then-ten-thousand for the whole shebang. Mr. Rock said that it was not worth anything but if she could get his pattern and formulas and his small stock it might be worth a few thousand dollars. He told Jacqulyn that she could not trust this fellow because his reputation followed him. "Make a deal and give him a small deposit and when he delivers what would be the inventory then you could go to the title company and you will put up the remainder money with the title company."

Mr. Rock thought that Shelly had the right ideas of using the perfume inventory as a base and told her to improve upon it. So, Jacqulyn had to be sure that the inventory was substantial enough in the formulas in her possession; otherwise, she should forget it as the other items like tables were relatively cheap and could be bought as a need to use commodity. So, he told Jacqulyn to call him if a sale was imminent and let him know what the perfume inventory was. She said she would do that so they locked up the warehouse and Jacqulyn and Mr. Rock had lunch with the crew at the studio.

Jacqulyn took orders for sandwiches, and she went to the deli. It was quiet now, so they were all enjoying their lunch and conversation. A bus pulled up and about twenty art students piled out of the bus into the studio. The art professor said that he would like for each of his students to have a personal credit account and that way, the student would be a customer and who knows, a force as a painter. So, Melissa prepared a simple credit application and used the master to produce twenty-five applications. She gave them a pen and told them to fill out their application. Mr. Rock and Jacqulyn stayed an extra hour to help with the influx of customers. The sales were small as they weren't buying anything but essentials to everyday needs for an artist. But they were budding painters and art students, so Constance's artwork brought out many. They all had inspirations to follow Constance's success. Probably out of the twenty, one might become a winner but for the others, it would be a lifetime of joy to be in the field of art for the rest of their lives as art had no prejudice. Art was like music. One did not have to be a singer to appreciate Nat King Cole or Judy Garland. One just had to appreciate good music.

Jacqulyn told Mr. Rock that she was leaving for her appointment with the perfume men. When she got there, he was all very anxious and smiling like he had his prey finally. Jacqulyn and he had been going about this sale for over six months now. So now is the time to expedite a yes on the deal. Jacqulyn noticed Mr. Perfume Man had an I-don't-care approach and his lack of enthusiasm showed now by his suggesting that maybe he would rather do this another time as she seemed to be a little preoccupied. He tried to mislead Jacqulyn that he needed the room for expansion but Jacqulyn saw the truth. His perfume operation could be put into a small square footage space as now it was spread all over. So again, she asked him for this inventory sheet which he claimed to have. Mr. Perfume Man asked his secretary to dig it up for him. Jacqulyn asked for 6 copies to be made. *Why in the world would she need six copies?* But he obliged. Jacqulyn placed three copies in front of her and got out her pen and as she read, she would put a price on the item. Perfume Man listed three Bunsen burners at one-hundred dollars apiece.

Jacqulyn scratched them out and wrote obsolete. Perfume Man said, "What do you mean obsolete? I just bought them."

Jacqulyn said that he was taken and that she just bought three with quick release. It was an auto lighting for fifty dollars each. She also volunteered to show him her paid receipt. She wasn't buying.

She did purchase three burners recently when she and Shelly were experimenting, but Mr. Rock added the hose and tank assembly that illuminated tapping into the hard gas line. It eliminated chances of a fire. Mister Perfume Man said he was not aware of that improvement, and he acknowledged that he got rooked. The perfume man has flashed at forty each whereas Jacqulyn said she bought six at ten dollars each. Each item was scrutinized and priced accordingly to her prices and not his. When she worked at Princess Perfume, she did all the buying, so she was aware of every price, and she plugged a ten percent raise. When it came to the fifty cases of twelve bottle perfumes on hand, she put *out of date* alongside so that that each bottle would have to be refilled and redacted. So possibly the whole lot was more bother than it was worth. Jacqulyn said she would make him one offer and expected him to say yes or no. So, she wrote two-thousand dollars cash which included the six pattern and formulas. He immediately said, "No — end of the meeting," and he left the room.

Jacqulyn packed her briefcase and left. When she got to the warehouse Mr. Rock said that perfume man agreed to the prize perfume and did not know he was talking to Mr. Rock as Mr. Rock did not identify himself. So, Jacqulyn said she would meet him at ten a.m. Mr. Rock said she did well as the fifty by twelve bottles of perfume would be a big savings of time as a base. Mr. Rock now had six formulas of his own that he had Shelly smell. They were labeled one through six and a formula card was placed along each bottle. So, Shelly started snipping. There was a space on the bottom of the formula card for comments. Shelly smelled number one and commented, "too mushy." Number two was sweet like perfume. Men probably wouldn't buy this. Number three was two vinegary. Number four was virtue. Number five was too mushy. Number six – "I think this is what I was looking for."

Mr. Rock said that he didn't go by smell. He was a chemist, but he said he thought that number six could be the answer, so he bottled a few to get out a sample and to get feedback. Amy liked it and Melissa said it was too strong. John said he would buy it. John set up a table outside the gone fishing restaurant and asked people to give their reaction. Out of one hundred people, sixty were favorable. Some said it was two perfumes but it was amazing that Shelly was quite close at the first run. Mr. Rock kept at it, but he did not neglect Melissa because when it was closing time, he closed his operation just as quickly. Next day, he went to the warehouse and John went to the red brick building.

Mr. Rock had only seen it from the outside and when John opened it up, Mr. Rock was in awe as it was huge. Mr. Rock and John estimated to bring each floor up to date and it would cost about two-hundred thousand dollars, plus passenger elevator that went up four storeys to encompass the large penthouse. Penthouse and elevator would need another million, so they were looking at a minimum of three million dollars. Jacqulyn said that they could remodel one floor at a time if they had a master plan. It would raise the ante but money would be less. So, the trio locked up and said there was plenty of time to ponder the remodel. The plan was to remodel and use the building as the headquarters for the deodorant business. Mr. Rock thought that it could be the red brick building that could be made into very usable medium. He also said that the second and third floor did not need to be as opulent as the first floor which greeted the buyers, but the elevator would have to be installed at the beginning or they would have to vacate the building because of the dust and working conditions. So, Mr. Rock went back to the chemistry end. Jacqulyn went back to check on the studio and she told Mr. Rock that she would be at the warehouse as soon as she talked to Shelly and Melissa. Amy had a long day so Melissa said she could leave early. John was still on his honeymoon, but he checked in with his secretary. His father started the real estate firm that he now owned. For 30 years, his father was at the same location. His father eventually bought the building.

John worked for his father from the time he was a senior in high school. People liked John; he was a people person — one of the top salespeople. His father had the foresight to set up a trust for John and his mother, Mrs. Bruno. John's mother never worked with the public. She was always a housewife, but she did help her husband with the bookkeeping as she spent two years in junior college and learned bookkeeping. John's father also had a CPA who did his taxes, and he did the firm's payroll. When John's father passed on, John became the owner with his mother. She passed on two years after her husband.

The firm under John's leadership was always one of the top realtors in the city. Antonia was John's aunt but at first, he and Mario did not see eye to eye on many things, so he very seldom went to the restaurant. John's other aunt lived in Florida and her son Paul was called his brother, but he really wasn't. Paul's father died and his mother remarried but Paul didn't like his stepfather, so he came to live with John and his mother. Paul went to live in the suburbs. He had a good business going as a handyman on a greater scale than some handyman. He could have been a licensed general contractor, but he preferred this lifestyle. John liked people but he was not a flashy guy. He preferred putting his energies into his real estate business but if he formed a friendship, it was usually solid. The bond between John and Mr. Rock was an example. John thought Mr. Rock was the best and Mr. Rock thought the same about John.

Eric came to visit, and he and Melissa talked about how well the studio was doing. Eric gave Melissa the money from the sale of Constance's 6 paintings which was exhilarating because it was so much money. A customer wanted to talk to Melissa, so Eric decided to look around the studio. Shelly was at the warehouse and Amy was not on duty yet so another customer approached Eric and asked if he was an employee. Eric told him he wasn't. *But could he possibly to be of any assistance?* He said probably not and that he would wait for Melissa to finish with her customer. Melissa came over to the customer and asked what he would like to see. It happened that the man was a freelance art auctioneer, and he was having an auction in two weeks in San Francisco, California. He said he was canvassing different art studios to see if they have an overabundance of any inventory that he might be able to auction off. Eric was all ears but did not interrupt. Melissa said that now she had nothing, but for the man to leave a card, which he did, and he left the studio. After the man left, Eric said to Melissa that he knew that man from somewhere, so he told Melissa that the same man had approached him at the New York studio, but he had a whole different gig that he was promoting. Eric was always on guard for fraud or robberies of art which were frequent, so he told Melissa that he had a gut feeling that something big was on the horizon — in this case, bad big.

So, he decided to call his detective friend in the Chicago Fraud Department. He explained to the detective, Jim Hershey, his feelings. He told Jim he had a business card that might have a good set of prints. Jim said that he would pick up the card and run it in the FBI fingerprint system. When the results came in, Jim told Eric that the man's name on the card was fake and the man had several encounters with the law, but they could only watch him for now as he hadn't done anything illegal regarding Eric's gut feeling. So for now it was shelved.

Eric noticed that Constance's eight by ten photos were not selling too well, or he assumed they were not selling well because they didn't occupy a prominent spot but were selected to a dark alcove in the studio. So, Eric asked Melissa, mostly out of curiosity, about the photographs and sure enough, Melissa said they were not a big seller. Eric pondered that for a while because in his studio in New York, photographs sold well whenever Constance painted anything — whether it was a still life or model or landscape. She always photographed the subject at about six or eight different angles before she painted the subject. So, Eric wondered if Constance had a landscape she painted and if the six or eight landscape photos pertaining to that landscape were removed from the picture box to a separate easel showing the photos and the actual paintings. Melissa thought it was worth a try. So, she and Eric picked out about 6 photo groupings. Shelly came in at that moment and greeted Eric with a big kiss and hug. Melissa showed Shelly the check for the fabulous amount of money for her modeling. Wow, if she could do those two or three times a year, wouldn't that be fantastic. Melissa showed Shelly what they were doing to try to promote the art photos. If they could inspire artists to adopt Constance's methods, they might their paintings in to be sold plus six or eight photos of the painting. Plus, the studio might develop a full-blown photography shop related to art. Constance thought that the six photos that she took before the actual painting gave her more insight into what the painting was all about, so she studied each photo carefully.

John stopped by and told him to take a lunch break and he thanked John and took his apron and said he was starved. Jacqulyn and John took orders in then went to fill the order. There she explained Eric's idea as promoting the photographs with the actual paintings and everyone agreed that it should work well. She passed the check around and that made everyone's day. Mr. Rock said that if he had that check he would take Melissa to Hawaii.

Then he said, "Check or no check, I'm going to take Melissa to Hawaii. Wow, Eric is here. Could you please try to arrange it?"

Everyone clapped. Someone said, "Does Eric have anything to say about this?"

Melissa said, "Hell no!"

Again there was laughter all around.

"Good for you, Melissa. You're the boss. Pull your rank on these miserable peons."

It must have been something in their lunch but suddenly, they all seemed relaxed and full of vigor. That's settled. Or was it settled?

Mr. Rock said he had another six deodorants for Shelly to smell so he and Shelly went back to the warehouse. This time they labeled each bottle ABC, etc. Up to twelve letters each bottle was to be graded one through ten so Mr. Rock said he would grade first then Shelly. After they were through, they brought in Jacqulyn and John. Lastly, they had Melissa and Eric and Amy smell each sample. It was kind of amazing, but Shelly again smelled the former number 6 plus Mr. Rock included another sample of number six and letters forms but this time he used the formula so that it was exactly like number six. Shelly had little hesitation when she picked number six again and it was above the letter B. If you picked number six and if you picked B, the consensus was favorable that six and B were probably as good a start as they could get. But Mr. Rock said it was too expensive to leave it at that because it would take thousands of dollars to get the right bottles and labels and whatever it took to make six B. They could set up a trial experiment in a city of choice and promote six and B but even that would entail thousands of dollars. Jacqulyn said she was willing to try the select city ideas and that might give them an idea what the public thought about a male deodorant. So, they proceeded and the city they picked was San Francisco, California because it was so cosmopolitan.

The name given to the deodorant was Switch. They proceeded to make large bottles of 6 and B. When all was ready, they would send advance teams to give out samples and get opinions from different ethnic groups. The results were more than what they anticipated. Department stores, large drug chains and the individual Mr. America endorsed the new product as a success but they never could keep up the demand out of that small warehouse so Mr. Rock said they would have to find a bottling plant with modern filling capacities. It could be small to medium in size, but it would have to be modern so that each bottle filled was the same. The modern assembly line would then label the bottles all automatically and humans at the end of the assembly would pack the deodorant twelve to a carton. The assembly plant did not need to necessarily be in San Francisco, the pilot city, but wherever it was, they needed rail services to it. Funding a bottling plant was put up to John as his realty firm covered all the United States listings. So, John located four or five potential choices — some for sale, some for rent and one that subbed their plant to different businesses.

So, Mr. Rock looked at what each was promoting. There was one small to medium plant that said they had to enlarge, but the whole assembly unit would have to be moved because they wanted to remain there but expand, adding to the present building. So, Mr. Rock called the plant superior who was also the engineer. Mr. Rock told the engineer that he did have an empty warehouse in Chicago, but it came down to the cost of starting from scratch or possibly faltering a plant that was in use. The engineer said that he could probably move the whole plant in Chicago and adapted to Mr. Rock's requirements. The engineer came to Chicago and met with Mr. Rock. He didn't see any obstacles. In fact, the site was perfect for his plan would only take up less of one-half of the second floor so there was room for expansion to even out the high cost of adding new building space as he was faced with. He then quoted Mr. Rock a guaranteed price of seven hundred and fifty thousand dollars, and he would set up his complete plant and adapt it to Mr. Rock's specifications. The engineer said that he would oversee the finished product to ensure a smooth transition. The only catch was that his plant could not be moved for two months, give or take, as they had commitments to fulfill. That was really a quest for Mr. Rock as he could remodel the first floor and put in the passenger elevator. So, he would get back to the engineer Jerry Subway in a day or so.

Mr. Rock talked to Jacqulyn and John and said that it looked like a steal as a new plant would cost between two or three million dollars. So, he proceeded to say that he would put up to one million dollars — not a loan, not a gift, but two million dollars would be theirs to work with. Then after five years he would consider how the money should be partialled. Mr. Rock said he didn't want any formal part of the business but if he was able and wanting to, he would enjoy helping them. Jacqulyn and John were grateful. Mr. Rock exposed fun or laughter in a business transition, but he couldn't resist. So, the seeds were sown and now the plant had to grow.

Mr. Rock said the very first thing would be for them to take measurements of the first floor and to draw up preliminary uses for the space. So, they bought some blueprint paper and each one was given a sheet to sketch up what they thought after they could modify or add to parts. So they had something meaningful developing. The free elevator was about three fourths back from the front doors so they all agreed that a wall would be erected at that point and the office to be on the first floor would be three fourths of the space and the one fourth in the back of the wall would be warehouse and loading and unloading dock. The freight elevator doors were in the warehouse side in the back of the freight elevator. They would have the passenger elevator that went from the basement to the penthouse. A six-passenger elevator would cost about a half a million dollars but was essential to the overall scheme of things.

When you enter the front doors there would be a receptionist desk with a modern phone system and three or four desks. The reception area would have a reasonable number of chairs and tables for magazines and the like. To the left would be two large executive suites. Scattered throughout would be cubicles for salespeople, bookkeepers, and the general staff. The general plan was adopted by all, but everyone was to keep in mind that they were encouraged to continue to preview the plan as changes or additions could be forthcoming.

The general construction was redoing the separation wall and the elevator shaft. Those were the most labor intensive. Once they were well along, the remainders would fall into place — messy and dusty but achievable. The front of the building was to be left rustic with the red brick, but the brick would be power washed. The entrance would also remain rustic as that was the charm that originally captured their attention. They adjourned for lunch.

Melissa told Jacqulyn that they were having a premium day. Artists were coming in and out. Customers that were not particularly art minded came in to browse and buy for someone in their place who were artistically inclined. Parents seemed to steer their adolescents into music and art. The parents beamed with great big smiles when their kindergarten artist brings home an art page with stick legged animals or people drawn on them. If it's an outline of a cow or a horse, they might have 10 or 15 colors on a horse and they never seemed to stay in the outline of the animal. They stuck the art to the side of the refrigerator to show everyone what a future artist's first work looked like. Mr. Rock with his labor of love kept plugging along and he told Melissa that no formula was perfect — that there was always room for change, but he was really pleased with the scent that Shelly had endorsed. Shelly also kept smelling and suggesting. She picked a scent that she thought would fit both genders.

The next day, the screaming headline said *Prominent Art Collector Robbed and is in Intensive Care*. It went on to say the collector and mega industrialist was abducted entering his elevator. Four men held him at gunpoint. When the elevator got to his apartment, they asked him to open his art vault and he said he could not because it was controlled by a clock. So, they backed him unconscious and threw him out the window. Even though it was only one story, he landed on a grouping of bushes and if he had not, he would have been dead. As it was, he was in bad shape. Unbeknownst to the thieves, the elevator had some electronics built into it that if more than one person went down or up to the apartment, a series of four hidden cameras recorded everything. If there were more than one person going up or down, the person with the key pushes the key past a certain notch and it would not record friendly visitors.

So, the police had something, but not much because they were mashed. But they had fingerprints and the police knew that they might have a suspect. The suspect was identified and picked up and confessed to all. He told the police that they stole all available art hanging on the walls or displays that were not in the vault. They sold all the paintings to an art studio in the Philippines. The local police raided the place and recovered most of the stolen works belonging to Mr. Chan plus there was stolen art from any number of unsolved robberies. The police lay the art on tables and let the press photograph them for the newspaper.

A movie mogul saw some of Shelly's modeling paintings by Constance and he liked what he saw. She was exceptionally beautiful, so he traced the newspaper pictures to Shelly in Chicago and Constance's studio D Art, so he flew to Chicago. He wanted to sign her up for a movie he was directing. The movie director went straight to Constance's studio and spoke with Melissa. She told him that Shelly was not here now, so Melissa asked the reason of his inquiry and he told her who he was, and that the movie studio had liked what he saw in the newspaper. So, the movie director was asked to locate Shelly and if he liked what he saw, to sign her up to a movie contract. The director happened to be in New York and after speaking with the police, Eric's name came up as this studio that sold the painting of Shelly to the billionaire industrialist, Mr. Chan. So, he went to see Eric at the studio. Eric was polite but would not divulge any information about Shelly without Shelly's approval. So, Eric stalled Mr. Jackson, the movie director, and he asked him to come back tomorrow. Mr. Jackson was furious. He asked Eric why he was being treated this way. He said he came in good faith so now it was Eric's turn to be furious. He told Mr. Jackson to leave and to not involve Shelly in any personal constraints without her permission. He also told Mr. Jackson that Shelly was a prominent person and there were many people who harassed her. At that Mr. Jackson, cooled off a bit, concerned with Eric that he could very well be someone he was not. He appreciated Eric's responsibility to his customers and employees as he assumed Shelly was a model contract to his studio. So, Mr. Jackson left and asked Eric to please contact Shelly as he had instructions from the head of the movie studio to sign her up as a movie star. Everything being equal, Eric called Melissa and explained the purpose of the call. Melissa hung up and told Shelly and Jacqulyn about the call from Mr. Jackson. So, Shelly and Jacqulyn and John discussed the matter and they all agreed that if Mr. Jackson was who he represented to be, there was no harm in listening to what he had in mind.

So, Jacqulyn called Eric and told him to check Mr. Jackson's credentials at the movie studio and if they were real, to tell Mr. Jackson that he could contact Shelly at this number. That was how he eventually got to see Melissa at the art studio. Melissa called Mr. Rock and told him that Mr. Jackson was here to talk to Shelly. Mr. Jackson was directed to go to the warehouse as they had a small room that Mr. Rock used as an office. Mr. Rock, John, Jacqulyn, and Shelly would be in a more private place than the art studio. So, they all sat around the desk that Mr. Rock used, and Mr. Jackson proceeded to explain his visit. Everyone there was in aprons or lab coats as they were all busy experimenting. Mr. Jackson was perplexed. He didn't know what to think. He imagined he would see a beautiful model all dressed to kill. Instead he saw a bunch of workers smelling of perfume. Shelly and Jacqulyn could be recognized as beautiful as they were. It would be hard for them to disguise themselves. They apologized to Mr. Jackson and explained that they were pursuing an eventful market of a product and that it required many tests and formulas that they all were involved in some form or another. What kind of model was he pursuing? So, Mr. Jackson could see that Shelly was as beautiful and well-proportioned as the paintings by Constance. He also thought that Jacquelyn could have been the mission he was on if Shelly were not there. So, he liked what he saw and signed a contract for a large sum of money, but John and

Mr. Rock said that Shelly was not to sign anything until Mr. Rock's attorney agreed with everything. Again, Mr. Jackson was baffled. Most aspiring actresses could not sign fast enough but this strange bunch beginning with Eric rebuffed his every move.

Strange. Mr. Jackson was again put off until tomorrow at one o'clock p.m. so they could confer with the attorney. It was approaching five days, but he thought Shelly would eventually be the star that the movie director and his superior thought she could be. So one day or five days was not the predominant pieces of the puzzle but part of the whole. John did not like the proposed idea because he believed that Jacqulyn would miss Shelly too much. After all Jacqulyn and Shelly saw each other every single day and now they would be separated, from Hollywood to Chicago. But Mr. Jackson made it clear that Shelly's part in the movie that he was directing would be short and he gave everyone there a small preview of what Shelly's sole role would be. He also said that the movie studio would pay Jacqulyn to be with Shelly for the three weeks Shelly would be tied up. Mr. Jackson said that he was unaware of any other plans the studio would have for Shelly.

So, the next day Mr. Jackson and Mr. Rock's attorney met in the same office with John, Mr. Rock and Jacqulyn. *What was it with these people? Did Shelly have to check in every time she had to go to the bathroom?* Good thing he just thought that and did not ask, or he might have found himself picking himself out of the gutter he was thrown in. So, Mr. Rock's attorney said he saw no real negatives to the contract. Shelly and Jacqulyn agreed the money was okay and the terms were that Shelly would be under contract for two years and would do two appearances per year. After two years they would renegotiate the contract, but Mr. Rock's attorney didn't like that, and he said that Shelly was to be able to accept any other offers for her services if they were presented. Mr. Jackson said he would have to get permission to accept that provision. Mr. Jackson got on the telephone and explained. The change was okay but this studio reserved the right to meet the intended offer. Mr. Rock's attorney agreed. Mr. Jackson signed an amendment that stated that fact. Shelly signed the contract and Mr. Jackson said that he would contact Shelly when he thought it was proper for her to appear in her first gig. So now Shelly was in a field that was full of great names and if she succeeded, was in a prominent class of talented people. Shelly was used to be in elite territory, but this was a step up. It was like being in the big leagues but on the second team. So, if something happened to a star she might be bumped up. Melissa often knew that Jacqulyn would not think of moving to another location, so the only option was to remodel the rear living quarters where Jack and Shelly lived. But now Shelly alone resided there because Jacqulyn got married. She and John lived in John's parents' house which was left to John. It was where John lived since he was born. When Jacqulyn and John married, they had the house remodeled while they were honeymooning in Reno. Shelly told Jacqulyn that if it was imperative, they remodeled to enlarge. She could live with Kelly if she did not already have a roommate. Kelly would have to have a roommate to help with expenses or she would have to downgrade. Shelly could rent an apartment of her own, but Jacqulyn said no. Melissa could live with that because it was just something that might have to be considered in the future.

John's realty business was moving in the right direction. What was making a difference was that many big corporations were transferring staff to meet their own influx of better times, so John's realty got a nice percentage of the transferring, seeking homes. The red brick building was doing fine. They were at the most disruptive part. Once the public elevator was in, the pace would be picked up. As of now it was imperative to rush things because Mr. Rock was adamant that the deodorant be one hundred percent before market time. As it was, Mr. Rock added and subtracted but Shelly's nose always picked up the changes and she would see no improvement over what they thought to be in the product. So, all the irons in the fire were going well. Jacqulyn and Shelly got a call from Mr. Jackson saying he would like Shelly to be on call.

He said that there were some 6 two-bedroom trailers available for the stars. That they did not have families and the stars stayed on site — Listening, going through, and reviewing stuff. So Jacqulyn and John and Shelly packed bags and went to Hollywood. Jacqulyn and John rented an apartment and Shelly moved into one of the trailers, but after her day's work was done, she would drive to Jacqulyn's and John's apartment and have dinner. Most evenings she would drive to the trailer especially if she had an early call. Sometimes she would be told that they would have a late start so Shelly would stay over in a separate small room that Jacqulyn and John made into a bedroom by buying a bed set and a couple pieces of furniture, and tables, and lamps. Jacqulyn figured the expense was minimal in comparison to not having Shelly there. After one week, John got a call that it was getting busy, and if he would consider coming back. He reluctantly did. So, Jacqulyn and Shelly were at the apartment alone. Another week went by with takes and retakes. The actual movie was recorded by the film crew with Mr. Jackson overseeing. The film technician was an older man name Charles Ritter. He fell madly in love with Shelly not like love birds but like father and daughter. So, he helped Shelly through rough spots and advised her about what to expect. He was an old timer, so it paid to listen.

The next day would be tough on Shelly. Jacqulyn was called back home due to something regarding decision-making at the art studio — a decision Melissa could not make. So, Jacqulyn went back home. There were three days left of shooting and Shelly would also be leaving. Everyone in the cast including Mr. Jackson was impressed at how mature Shelly was in all her scenes. Shelly was terrific and no one was more happy than old Mr. Ritter but he knew it from the word go because he recorded everything on film and with the instant replay, he could determine within minutes of the shoot that it was a go or had to be retaken.

Shelly had just finished for the day and went to the trailer to shower and freshen up. She just got out of the shower when Mr. Ritter said that that she should come and see the replay — that it's fantastic. So Shelly poked her head out the door and said that she would be there in a few minutes. Shelly went over to where Mr. Ritter was winding some film on a spool. He stopped what he was doing and turned on the instant replay that was projected on to a portable screen. Shelly thought it was good, but she was not an authority. But Mr. Ritter was, and he told Shelly that she was a natural and that in all his years he had never seen a novice perform so professionally. He couldn't stop praising her during the instant replay, but Shelly had enough. She kissed the old man on the cheek and playfully punched him on the shoulder and said flattery will get you everywhere and she started to leave. Theset seemed to have big electrical cables on the floor, running to equipment all over the place. Shelly stepped over this one cable that was frayed and they shot electrical sparks. They came out like starburst and before the GFI current breaker could click off she was burned very badly. But it was a shock of the sparks flying everywhere that caused Shelly to jump back. As she did, she landed on a big cord that rotated and caused her to fall. There was a chair there that she was reaching for when the cord rolled her foot over again and Shelly put the sharp edge of the chair smacked on her temple, causing a big deep cut, spitting blood all over. She was unconscious.

Mr. Ritter saw the whole accident enfolding but was too slow to react. He immediately called 911 and an ambulance was dispatched to the scene. The movie lot had a nurse station right around the corner, but the doctor had left for the day. A nurse came running up and she tried to bring Shelly back to consciousness but to no avail. She wrapped up Shelly's arm, trying to stop the flow of blood. The ambulance arrived and set up a portable blood transfusion. One of the emergency people thought that she busted an artery and was drowning in her own blood as blood was coming out of all the orifices in her head. They had no fixes for anything that volatile so all they could do was rush her to a hospital where brain specialists would have to operate immediately. While they were loading Shelly, the senior ambulance man called the hospital and instructed that a team of brain surgeons be on hand. He said that the victim was unconscious, but she had a pulse, and he gave them a number. On the small portable lifeline, the ambulance showed the brain was slowing down quickly.

The ambulance arrived at the hospital, and she was rushed into surgery. They opened her head to relieve the pressure and discovered she had a massive blood leak. They clamped the suspected artery. That helped a little, but her pulse was slipping badly as the brain was not functioning properly. She was now pronounced to be in a coma. No one was able to relax because clamps had to be opened and closed. The danger of shock was very prevalent. If she entered extreme shock, it could all be over. While the medical people were trying to save her life, someone called Mr. Jackson and the interned called Jacqulyn. Jacqulyn and John and Mr. Rock flew to Hollywood. Shelly was still in a coma and the head doctor of the hospital told Jacqulyn that Shelly would be a paraplegic at the least if she came out of the coma.

Right now, the lifesaving machines were probably the only thing keeping her alive. Jacqulyn fainted and Mr. Rock caught her before she hit the floor. Mr. Ritter, the cameraman, had a talent bridge photography that led him into a life of fantasy and lewdness which got him in trouble with the law from time to time. He would photograph young runaways needing money, mostly teens. So now he had this good job with this movie studio as a cameraman and he wasn't going to blow this because he was getting too old to start again. But all habits die hard so he used his camera in the wee hours of the morning. He photographed the actions being played out in the hotel across the street, developed the film, and sold the stills to unethical act dealers for photo shop stealing and such unsavory practices. The money he made paid for his excessive drinking and drug habits.

One such dealer got wind of the fact that he had a new girl at the studio who was a knockout, so they pressured him into getting some photos of her. Mr. Ritter knew Shelly would not go for anything unethical, so he had to photograph her when she was least expecting being photographed. This day he called for Shelly to see her replay of the days filming. He thought he might get some unexpected shots of her coming out of the trailer for dinner. Sometimes the worst unethical people walk out. After Shelly saw the replay and they talked about her future and films, she started to go back to the trailer. Mr. Ritter photographed her coming to the camera location. Mr. Ritter would disconnect the light so that when he put the camera on automatic it was filming but only where it was pointed at as he could not be in the back of the camera in live mode. If he pointed the camera at them, they would know they were being photographed. So, he was a sly fox and he set his camera on widefield and pointed it to read the trailer and he would be away from the camera so as not to arouse suspicion. So, every step Shelly took towards the trailer was being photographed. Then the unexpected happened when she stepped on the frayed wires. He completely lost track of his filming and went to help Shelly as he was witnessing the whole accident plus the camera was photographing the whole accident. He called 911 and was called a hero in the paper for his perseverance of mind and awareness that Shelly needed assistance and fast. So, he had millions in the camera but he wondered how he could capitalize on it. If he held back the film, he could be charged with withholding information because he knew that lawyers were going to exploit the whole thing seeing that the wires were frayed causing the hot sparks to set up the fall.

Jacqulyn stayed at Shelly's bedside. She wouldn't leave but John and Mr. Rock went back to tend to business. John said he would check on things after reality and fly back. Three weeks went by and

Shelly was still in a coma. The doctor said there was little hope and they suggested Jacqulyn give permission to take her off the machines that were keeping her alive. Mr. Rock being older and more practical told John that Jacqulyn should get a lawyer and sue the movie studio for negligence because of the way the electrical lines were running all over on the floor plus some were in bad condition. John told Mr. Rock that he would talk to Jacqulyn, but he knew she was too emotionally involved. She didn't consider money when it came to her little sister. She was her only concern. Mr. Rock tried to convince John. The damage was done, and the movie people were responsible and negligent only because to them it was all about money. The movie people hired expensive lawyers who were on retainers plus others that were hired outright for one case or another. Being a big-time studio, they had issues constantly with actors and actresses. The latest suggested to their movie people to play a raining game and not open a can of worms prematurely. When and if the time came that Jacqulyn was stable enough, they then could face whatever it was to face. Mr. Rock wouldn't let loose, and John was the only person he had contact with, seeing that Jacqulyn would not leave Shelly. She cared for Shelly a lot, but she felt that being an employee, it was not her place to make any decisions of a personal nature. But she said that Mr. Rock looked at Jacqulyn and Shelly as surrogate daughters. John finally connected and said he would talk to Jacqulyn, but he knew he was walking on eggs and had to approach the matter carefully only if the occasion came up.

So, John talked to Jacqulyn one day when Jacqulyn said that if the movie people were not irresponsible that Shelly would not be where she was. That gave John a little window of opportunity, so he told Jacqulyn that Mr. Rock suggested that she hire his attorney to negotiate for her. John was amazed she said yes. So, Mr. Jenkins, who was Mr. Rock's attorney, was hired. The very first thing he did was contact the movie people's attorneys to discuss the possibilities of a settlement or forced to file suit against the movie people. Mr. Hayward was the CEO of the large movie studio bearing his name as he inherited the movie business from his father before it became a public company. He was elected CEO by the board when they went public. Mr. Hayward's attorney said that they would bring the matter up with Mr. Hayward and the board of directors. A special meeting would have to be scheduled. Mr. Rock's attorney, Mr. Jenkins said that he would like a response. Mr. Jenkins went to the public Police Department and asked to see the police report. He also talked to the chief of security for Hayward studios. They also submitted a report to the studio.

One person who was mentioned in all reports was Mr. Ritter as he was the only eyewitness to Shelly's accident. There was no mention of a film in either report. Mr. Jenkins talked to Mr. Ritter who was on a medical leave of his job claiming that this accident he witnessed was so traumatic that he could not do his job properly. Mr. Jenkins went to Mr. Ritter's home to talk to him; he also submitted a report to the two police departments. Jenkins had a copy. He talked to Mr. Ritter, and he noticed that Mr. Ritter was very uncomfortable and that at times he would lose his train of thought and his speech was slurred like he was on alcohol or drugs. So, Mr. Jenkins felt Mr. Ritter needed further looking into. Mr. Jenkins hired a private investigating company to deal with the issue of Mr. Ritter. A report from the investigator came to him that Mr. Ritter was seeing this photo studio many times, so they had to try to find out why. The investigating firm sent a female investigator to the photo studio and she pretended that she wanted some off the wall pictures and if they could accommodate her. She was willing to pay the going rate. She said she was particularly interested in car accidents. "Some accidents are not as gory, but they tell a tale — like being shot or strangled. I have a client that buys my stuff and without pictures I cannot make my money."

So, the owner of the shop thought it was worth a try. She handed the owner a card and said, "You know, that's not my real name."

They both laughed. Two days later, she got a call: "Come and see me — Praise Photo Shop. When she got there, the owner of the shop said that he had some pictures. They weren't exactly gory although the result could be traumatic. *Would you be interested? The price is not cheap because it pertains to a high-level personality.* There was a series of eight photos that could not be broken up and the price would be forty thousand dollars and it would not be negotiable. The owner said he would get back to her. So, it was left like that but to Mr. Jenkins it looked promising especially that it was a prominent person. So, they just had to wait.

In Chicago, things were really going well on the renovation of the red brick building although that was not the center of attraction that it was a short while back. Shelly's condition had everyone involved, with Shelly's past in a funk. Melissa, Amy, and Mr. Rock, and of course, John — could they pull out of this? Jacqulyn was young. If she set her mind to putting the tragedy behind her, she could. But conversely it could break her. John thought that Jacqulyn's behavior so far was that nothing mattered anymore. She told John that she loved him very much, but Shelly was her life. John just made it better. John and Mr. Rock knew it was going to get worse. Could Jacqulyn be able to bite the bullet and let Shelly free? If God intervened, she would have no choice, but for her to have to say *do it* was problematic. Did she have the stomach for it? Counseling might help. All they knew was that they would not like to be in Jacqulyn's shoes. The art studio, although shrouded in gloom, was doing especially well. So, that was good for Amy and Melissa as they didn't have as much time to dwell on the accident. John's Realty was doing well also. They seemed to be steady as they went year in and year out. Mr. Rock reached a point where the core product was developed in the lab as much as it was going to be, but they needed more than one product to succeed. This product was a sole one. Spray — also some product that would be his and hers in one container. If Shelly were here, she would save them hours of mixing and testing as she was a walking lab. Her nose or smell would skip by many tedious trials and errors. Wishful thinking would not bring her to the lab ever again. Mr. Rock was a breed above other chemists. He needed motivation like most people do. Who is that Princess? His motivation was his chemist wife? She would have an idea, or he would have an idea and they would both try to develop it. It was much harder now since he was alone and if something popped up, he could not share it. Because they were not chemists, the experiment might go in the garbage although it might have been worth chasing. Mr. Rock thought if he had a good chemist working beside him, he might improve. In any event they would have to hire someone eventually — so why not now.

In the art studio Amy seemed to be indispensable as she graduated from basic art to advanced. She was not the prettiest artist so she could not do modeling or such so she concentrated on being the best she could. Already her name is getting around as Melissa sold some of her paintings. Melissa, being an appraiser, figured that she was above all and in a few years would be in the elite class. Melissa would not pull any punches regardless of how much she liked Amy. Amy either had it or didn't but happily Melissa thought she didn't have to be a quality artist with a fine following.

John's brother Paul recently hired an apprentice carpenter who had two years of chemistry at Davis in California. It was a prominent school but due to financial problems, he had trouble resorting to another medium to make a living, hence, carpentry. One day John and Paul were having dinner together and Paul's wife was visiting some relatives on the East Coast and of course Jacqulyn was with Shelly. They discussed business among other things and John said that Mr. Rock needed an assistant chemist, so Paul told him about Darrell and that he claimed to have two years of college chemistry. Darrell's business was slowing down due to the extreme weather, and he was going to have to find other work. *Could Mr. Rock use him?* He said Darrell was very punctual and learned fast. So, John told Paul that he would pass the information to Mr. Rock which he did. Mr. Rock thought that he would like someone more advanced. He would interview Darrell. Mr. Rock interviewed Darrell and soon discovered that Darrell had it in him to be a chemist but that he had a lot to learn. But if someone was looking for a potential trainee Darrell would fit the bill. So, Mr. Rock figured that he was in need of an assistant today and he did not especially need years of experience so he could wait for the right person to come along. In the meantime, Darrell would do just fine.

Mr. Rock hired Darrell and suggested that the young man continue his education with evening classes and possibly weekend classes. Darrell was very anxious to begin working again in the chemistry field and especially for someone as prominent as Mr. Rock but as always there was a catch. Darrell lived with friends in the Chicago suburb, and they shared expenses. So, the dilemma was solved temporarily by Mr. Rock telling Darrell he could live in the back end of the warehouse that was flimsily partitioned off by some former tenant. It was probably used as a lounge area, and it was connected to the bathroom areas. Seeing that Darrell was single and very little in the way of financial security, it would suffice temporarily. Mr. Rock gave Darrell advancements on his first two weeks salary as Darrell needed to settle accounts with his former roommates.

The lady investigator agreed to meet with Ray if he was the Ray's Photo and Portrait owner but Ray being especially cautious, did not want to end up in prison, so he had one of his associates follow her every move. Mr. Jenkins told Amber, the lady investigator, to not go to her regular apartment, but rent a motel room and stay there until the investigation was over. The tail was always taken to the motel. Furthermore, Amber was to never contact him or ever phone him as her phones might be tapped by both sides. Amber was given another prayer that night — work to enhance her credibility. The prop was a cheap briefcase but inside were three envelopes with lewd pictures and money in each envelope and they were marked *C. F. G. Find the front* — also some loose photos all pertaining to sex deviants, etc. So, when she went to see Ray, she was to "accidentally" leave her briefcase behind on the floor or chair that she might sit on waiting. The reason was that while Ray took Amber to a small office to show her pictures someone would carefully investigate the contents of the briefcase. Sure enough, what happened was they were not in the office very long when the telephone extension phone rang. Ray didn't say much — just yes and cryptic talk — but the prop did the trick. Ray was being chatty as if he were stalling waiting to hear from the results of the prop. After the call, Amber noticed a distinct businesslike attitude. So, Ray went to a small safe embedded in concrete in the floor and he pulled out an envelope and laid eight pictures on the desk. He said that they were pictures of an actress that was very critical in the hospital and the pictures were not especially gory, but they showed distinctly the sparks and frayed wire. Ray said that all the evidence of the accident had been cleaned up by the special security people working for the Hayward Movie Studios. The accident occurred after the normal working hours so there was no witness since except the cameraman who got lucky and photographed the accident. Ray said the pictures could be sold to either party, or both, for thousands. Amber pretended to be interested but said that her clients were not exactly in that type of market, but she might have a client who specialized in blackmail and other illegal schemes as she would contact them. In the meantime, she needed the illicit sex and gory stuff staff to call her. Amber was experienced enough to suspect that she might be followed and watched — her every move very closely. So a meeting was arranged for her to get on a train and sit in a designated seat that had one of Mr. Jenkin's men sitting at. She was not to talk to the man except to say hello as someone could be there recording any conversations. She was to slip her findings to the passenger and leave at a convenient stop that the train made. Amber was good and after a day of waiting, she endeavor to lose her tails and meet Mr. Jenkins in a motel. In disguise, she was confident that she probably lost the tails for they were probably not experienced people. Mr. Jenkins waited a week. Ray explained that she could not make a deal with her people, so the deal was off. Mr. Jenkins waited another week then he moved fast. He waited for Mr. Ritter to enter his apartment then he knocked and addressed himself as Ray. The door was immediately unlocked as Mr. Ritter thought this was his lucky day. Mr. Jackson and two of his associates burst into the room and strong-armed Mr. Ritter to sit and listen. Mr. Jenkins said, *twenty years in prison for concealing evidence and trying to sell evidence for his gain and further derail future, legal proceedings.* They had a proof meeting with Ray's Photo Studio with the sole purpose of blackmailing. Mr. Richard could tell the plot was exposed and Mr. Jenkins knew too much, and it was not theory. So, Mr. Ritter asked what they wanted, and Mr. Jenkins told Mr. Ritter he wanted the roll of film — all the individual pictures that were developed. Mr. Ritter did not know if these people were FBI, police, or what, as Mr. Jenkins did not formally introduce them. So, Mr. Ritter asked what would happen to him and Mr. Jackson said that they would do everything they could to not complicate Mr. Ritter any more than necessary. So, Mr. Ritter foldedback a piece of carpet and removed two floorboards and there lay ten or fifteen rolls of film and hundreds of photos. Mr. Jenkin's associates took over and moved Mr. Ritter out of the way. A pillowcase was removed from its cushion and everything in the cachet were put in the pillowcase and there were also stacks of one-hundred-dollar bills with rubber bands around them. Mr. Ritter was crying. Mr. Jenkins took one stack of bills and threw it on the bed for Mr. Ritter. Mr. Jenkins had someone he used to develop the rules and what he saw was exciting him enough that he kept saying *got you* to nobody in particular. Hayward and his attorneys were alleging that Shelly stumbled and they admitted that she could have stumbled on a cord, but nobody would never be one hundred percent sure about that. But they were willing to give Mr. Jenkins the benefit of the doubt and settle for this sum or they would go to court. Mr. Jenkins said that Mr. Ritter was an eyewitness and conceded to the police exactly what happened about the frayed electrical cord and the burning shoots of hot sparks that caused the accident. Since then Mr. Ritter denied everything and said he was coerced by the city police and the security police. He claimed he asked for legal attorney but was ignored. Mr. Ritter had a very bad police record. He had to weigh his every move so that he didn't land himself into another twenty years behind bars. So, Mr. Jenkins took out a bundle of photographs — all stamped not originals — and laid them on the table for Mr. Hayward's attorney. The attorneys were bright enough to see: if they went to court someone was going to be in big trouble as to why evidence was removed. The security police blamed the chief. The chief would play Mr. Hayward who was on top of it all. Someone paid Mr. Ritter for his testimony. All in all, Mr. Jenkins had them by the proverbial you-know-what. They had to ask Mr. Jenkins what he would expect if they settled, and Mr. Jenkins told them he would meet with them tomorrow same place, one p.m.

So, Mr. Jenkins phoned Mr. Rock and John and told them where they were. Mr. Jenkins told them to fly, that they needed to talk, and they all had to be ready in case they had to sign papers. That evening, Mr. Jenkins, Mr. Rock, John, and Jacqulyn had dinner and went to the hotel to plan. Jacqulyn said that she could not see how they could proceed while Shelly was still in a coma. Mr. Jenkins said that they could settle and leave that part. There would be a minimum of them paying all medical costs, all attorney fees and any additional amount to be negotiated. Mr. Rock told Mr. Jenkins to stall the prearranged meeting and they might want to debate it further. Mr. Jenkins would and did the next morning, but he also told Mr. Rock and company that *you saw the negotiations in progress sometimes fire back at them as they also have an opportunity to further ponder their decision. Or something might break in their favor like it did with us and Mr. Ritter.* Mr. Jenkins said it behoove them to be prudent if they wanted to settle because it appeared they want to settle. So, it was left as is and the discussions would come.

Jacqulyn was told by the hospital that comas usually lasted about two weeks and if they persisted, they were usually in a negative state, waiting for the inevitable to happen or possibly disconnect from the machines. So already it's been well past the two weeks and there was no sign of improvement, and the severity of the accident was such that the brain scans and CT scan showed from the start that they were fighting an uphill battle. Usually with the coma or prolonged need for the machines, the ultimate losers are the relatives that could not or would not bring closure to the inevitable. Mr. Jenkins suggested that knowing those facts and the fact that Shelly was past the point of return, we could place a figure on the settlement and end the agony. Mr. Jenkins did not want to be so blunt but sometimes it was the only way for people to react to traumatic experiences. *Llife is not life but in everlasting prolonged sorrow. When it gets to that point, money — any amount — is not the answer. It usually takes a divine experience to prompt these people to act intelligently and not emotionally. So money does matter. It cannot bring back what is lost but money, if not needed exactly, can be donated to charities to help future victims of comas, brain concussions, and related injuries or sicknesses. So don't say you don't care about the money because it can help somewhere along the line.*

So, they took Mr. Jenkin's advice and programmed everything into the settlement and called for another meeting for tomorrow if convenient. The attorneys were available, but Mr. Hayward was leaving for Europe tomorrow, and he would not be there. His instructions were to do whatever was best for Hayward Movie Studios and he would agree. The next day the attorneys met, and it was sweet and supple. They agreed, paperwork signed, and a check was presented. The next day Jacqulyn signed to let Shelly go in peace. She, Jacqulyn, would never be the same but it was the most merciful decision. Jacqulyn probably could never laugh or live normally again without feeling some guilt. While she was happier, smiling, it was going to be hard physically. Doctors throughout the world have patients with extreme depression and remorse about different issues. Doctors' biggest concerns were to protect them from themselves such as suicide or some bodily injury. It was usually too deep for doctors to assess so they kept looking for answers.

The whole crew left Hollywood to do the tasks at hand in another world or so it seems. John was instructed by the doctors that the best therapy for Jacqulyn was to keep her involved in anything and not let Jacqulyn lie around and feel sorry for herself and try to always have people she loved around her. They called it therapy but whatever word was used or whatever was done usually depends on the person herself.

Jacqulyn was never a very demonstrative person. It seemed she was always one step from falling into a big, cavernous hole, and just when she and Shelly were starting to see some daylight. Calamity befell them so Jacqulyn would always be aware of that. Jacqulyn and Shelly were both liked by others, but Jacqulyn had to try harder to achieve that where it came very natural for Shelly. Jacqulyn had too many responsibilities at too young an age to be completely complete. Most girls at fourteen partied or slept over with their friends or went to the beach. Jacqulyn probably never went to a friend's birthday party or another function as she was always steady.

Jacqulyn before the accident begged Mario to get a new girl to work evenings as she wanted to be with Shelly in Hollywood. So at least John and Jacqulyn could share their evenings together. The studio was doing so well that Melissa said that they could open the doors and let the place operate by itself. John said that the red brick building was her inspiration and he thought that she should be involved in what was going on because whatever was going on was not as personal as her feelings of what was going on. For instance, the elevator shaft was completed. Electrical conduit was installed so we come to the actual elevator. It's personal and Jacqulyn should give it her touch so that it was not a drab thing that went up and down, but it was well lit — nice colors, state of the art control system. If it was left to others, it wouldn't be a friendly elevator but a workhorse. Jacqulyn must tell the engineers to only go three stories to get to the penthouse. It had to have some mechanism to override so they could go to the penthouse, but it could not be accessible to the public — same as going to the basement. The actual basement was so full of boilers and motors. If the public had access to the basement, unreliable people could exploit it to the point of using it to commit personal mayhem or vandalism or even terrorist acts. So, it was important to look ahead and address certain possibilities.

Jacqulyn was up to it, and she said that she wanted to get back into the harness and see if the old habits would come back to her. One thing that came back positively was seeing Mark, Rio, and Antonio and Hans and especially eating Han's spaghetti and meatballs with John and Mr. Rock and Melissa. It seemed a long time ago, but it was only a short time ago. So, they all thought Jacqulyn was pulling out of it. They had to be careful that Jacqulyn did not get the feeling that she was being pampered. The idea would be that Jacqulyn found her place again naturally. So, she jumped right in and helped Mr. Rock and met Darrell. Then she would run over to Melissa and Amy. Melissa was busy so she hired Kelly full-time, and Kelly seemed to fill the void that Shelly left as she was a model, and she also was a capable salesperson, but everyone was very careful to not let Jacqulyn hear that Kelly was replacing Shelly. It would have to come to Jacqulyn naturally which it did one day. She went to the studio, and she didn't see Kelly. Melissa said that Kelly was on a modeling assignment, and she held her breath. Jacqulyn said that was good, that eventually they should probably have two or three girls doing that. In fact, maybe part of the living space could be remodeled. So, she asked Melissa if she still wanted to expand, and Melissa said empathetically yes.

Jacqulyn left to have lunch with John. Melissa could not wait to call Mr. Rock and tell him about how Jacqulyn reacted when she was told that Kelly was out modeling. Mr. Rock said that it was a positive sign and that Jacqulyn would make it. Jacqulyn and John had lunch and Jacqulyn asked John if he would have time to help her tomorrow to take measurements and help plan the floor layout. He said fine. Jacqulyn continued, "Now that Shelly and I are not living there, the only logical thing to do would be to expand it into the living quarters. Leasing it to a family was out of the question."

Right off the bat John thought Jacqulyn was already healing at a good normal pace and hopefully it would continue. Jacqulyn understood people were treating her with knit gloves, and she appreciated that so many cared for her. Jacqulyn said to herself, *Shelly is gone but I must live and hold up my end of everything. It will be hard, but I can do it.*

The next day, she and John went to breakfast and made small talk. After breakfast they drove to the studio. Melissa was ready to go. Jacqulyn told Melissa that she and John were there to take measurements and see how they could incorporate the former living quarters that Jacqulyn and Shelly shared. Melissa gave Jacqulyn an artist tablet and they worked until noon, measuring and verifying measurements. When it was lunchtime, John and Jacqulyn drove to the deli and ordered sandwiches and soft drinks. At lunchtime Mr. Rock and Melissa closed the warehouse so that Mr. Rock could have lunch with Melissa. Melissa observed that Darrell and Amy usually sat near each other and marched to a different time than the rest of the crew. Darrell was a year older, but Amy was far more mature than Darrell. Mr. Rock said he was trying hard, and he would eventually be a good chemist. Darrell had a chance to really establish himself with Mr. Rock and maybe take over for when Mr. Rock decided that the deodorant venture was going smooth enough for him to leave. He told John that he would like to marry Melissa and buy a house on Maui, and commute between Maui and the mainland where he thought he would buy a house. The house n Chicago on Lake Michigan would be their main home and use Maui as a sort of vacation or getaway sort of home. When he and Melissa were not there, members of the crew could go there and spend a week or two and happily let the rest of the world go by.

At the red brick building, the passenger elevator was up and running as it was a work of art. The separation wall was in, and all the offices were framed and painted. The only thing left to do on the first floor was to put down the floor covering, then dust and clean. In the meantime, the engineer said he was ready to install the automatic bottling plant. The work on the second floor would be done from the back of the building which had a huge loading platform and use the freight elevator to take the parts to the second floor. So, they began working on their project and the engineer figured if everything went right, they should have it running in two months. Mr. Rock was elated.

The male deodorant sample program was working a little too fast as they were already getting orders from various mediums. The only thing Mr. Rock could do was to put them on hold and the firms that couldn't wait or did not want to wait would either be lost or come back when they were more organized. Mr. Rock thought to have an emergency backup. If Mr. Rock could not perform once that the plant opened, it would still be opened and not on a hit or miss schedule, but every day if itneeded productions. So, Mr. Rock told Darrell that along with his chemistry, he was to learn the business of bottling techniques as it was huge. The bottles of every product being filled moved fast, from billing to packing. So the plant engineer must be always on his toes while the production was taking place. One bottle that accidentally toppled could cause a serious problem. So, the engineer must be able to shut down at a second's notice. Darrell was assured that he would not regret the decisions of learning something other than chemistry plus the fact that he would be given a nice raise. Darrell also liked Mr. Rock enough to follow his every advice. Darrell already was in debt to Mr. Rock for helping him financially after Paul let him go. Incidentally Paul said that it was his business that was in a slump so Darrell would not have been working and as everyone attested, the bills and obligations did not stop; they just kept rolling along.

Mr. Rock started to build a big reserve of deodorant so when the time came, they could still fill a great quantity of orders. If the occasion arose and someone booked orders of deodorant with bottles, a fresh supply would be produced. The quantity would be less so Mr. Rock estimated he could keep up with the demand. In any business if the inventory gets too low or even too high the company in question loses. In the stock market, if you have too much inventory then it means your business is not selling to capacity. If you have too little inventory, the analysts assume you do not have enough capital to keep the inventory to capacity. So, every business is always trying to determine the direction their industry is going. Do you have to keep your fingers on the pulse always? So that was Mr. Rock's most ardent problem. If Mr. Rock manufactured too much deodorant it could go stale and must be discarded. Is the manufacturers made too little, they might not be able to keep up with demand. Some owners like to think the latter is better but it is not because a dealer needs his goods And if you can't supply then he loses faith in your company and might take his business elsewhere. Don't ever get complacent and think the customer will wait because there is always another company that is hungry enough to do anything to get your shelf space, even lose money for a while to entice the customer to buy your product.

Out of nowhere Jacqulyn told John that she wanted to go full steam ahead on the constant studio enlargement. The studio was slated to close for two weeks for vacation so that would give them two full weeks to get a jump start on the expansion. Jacqulyn also discussed with John the possibility of closing one week earlier — the reason being a closing for remodeling to open agai inn three weeks. John thought it was reasonable, so Jacqulyn and John advised the staff of their decision. Melissa was thankful as she was tired and could use a nice long retreat from her everyday routine that she established to get Constance's studio to a good start. Kelly would just relax and take on some modeling work if it came along. Mr. Rock and Darrell were not able to enjoy any form the vacation time. In fact, their workload increased substantially as the process neared completion for the deodorant company to launch their product. The closer the physical aspect of the venture approached meant that Mr. Rock had to be ready with the product that was the actual deodorant. Jacqulyn and John would not have any respite as now they would have to ensure a smooth remodel to Constance's studio so they could reopen again in three weeks. Jacqulyn was adamant that the studio be modeled before the deodorant debut because of the advertising and presales pitch. John suggested that Paul take on the task of remodeling Constance's studio.

Paul's construction company still sometimes happens in construction. Try as you may even buy a job. Homeowners just weren't spending money right now. Why? The economy couldn't be blamed as it was not robust but there were no real or imagined slowdowns. No, it was just a phase that was happening and until it broke you just waited. So, Paul was grateful to Jacqulyn and John. The biggest and most significant part of the remodel was to ensure that the thousands of dollars' worth of paintings and other inventory be protected from the dust and related aspects of all remodels. So, John suggested that they hire a professional moving company to bring in two large moving bands and move the bulk of the paintings to the moving van. Then the van would be moved to the company's lot. The paintings were free from the mess of the remodeling, but it was not quite that simple as Jacqulyn had to put a five-million-dollar insurance writer on the paintings. Plus, she had to hire twenty-four hours security to protect the paintings from theft. The paintings had to be protected as that was the reason for Constance's studios' existence. Paul figured the wall separating the studio from the living quarters would remain until all of the work in the living quarters were done. Then Paul would use plastic and masks to minimize the dust to and from the newly remodeled living quarters in the existing studio. So, in essence, the Paul had two temporary plastic walls, one on each side of the separating wall that had to be removed by opening a hole in the exterior wall of the building. Paul was able to put a large debris box close to the opening and remove the plaster insulation and two by four out of the building. It was accomplished much easier than Paul imagined. The wall was removed, and patching was done, and Paul then brought in a troop of professional people who had special equipment to control dust and they would remove the plastic walls.

It was amazing that now the studio was one and one fourth larger than it was previously but to the untrained eye it appeared as if the remodel never happened. New floor coverings were laid. Modern lighting was installed, and it was now ready to bring back the paintings and other inventory and to also restock or add stock because of the expansion. Melissa, Amy, and Kelly would now use their revitalized bodies to reset all the easels and paraphernalia that would enhance the paintings. The remodel took one week longer than expected but the result exceeded all expectations. So, Jacqulyn decided to advertise the reopening and invite the public to coffee and other refreshments plus have a free drawing and the lucky person was to have a three-day-all-expense-paid trip to an amusement park, including three days and nights in a luxury hotel. The opening was a huge success.

Melissa kiddingly told Mr. Rock that now that they were off and running again that maybe they should close again and get another breather. So, Jacqulyn suggested she call Eric and have him come down with a couple of his assistants and kind of fill in so Melissa and Amy and Kelly could have a few more days off but not necessarily all at once. The extra days off accomplished miracles because everyone was beat. Now, they could operate efficiently as they were now rested. Melissa said that she hoped to never have to go through that traumatic experience again.

So they were back to the deodorant. About the expansion of the studio, Eric and Melissa said that the actual business looked to be doubled and if it continued God only knew what they would do. Jacqulyn said no more and said it was what it was. One day Melissa opened the studio doors to begin her day. A sideways glance observed an Asian girl in a wheelchair. Melissa continued opening locks as there were four in all. The locks were part of the security system and were mandatory for this security system to function at one hundred percent. She was concentrating on getting the lock correctly punched in as each lock had a different code. All four locks operated as one if all codes were correct. If a wrong code was punched in, the doors would not open. The Asian girl realized that Melissa was concentrating and politely waited until she finished doing her thing. The Asian girl realized Melissa finished her concentration because she opened the door to enter the studio. The girl wheeled towards Melissa and politely asked if she could speak with Jacqulyn. So, she opened the door wide and let the girl in and she again asked to speak to Jacqulyn. Melissa told her that Jacqulyn would not be in for another hour but if it was urgent, she could try and reach her. The girl said that she wouldn't want to impose on Melissa's generosity. She said she would wait for Jacqulyn. Melissa asked her if she would like to have some coffee, or a beverage or water and the girl said she would be thankful for a cup of coffee. Melissa excused herself while she went to the kitchen to brew some coffee. Directly Amy came in followed by Kelly and they were officially open. Melissa brought the girl a cup of coffee and asked if she wanted cream and sugar. The girl apologized and said she was being a nuisance but would like both. She said that she could wheel to the kitchen and help herself.

Melissa said it was no problem as she set up coffee every morning for the early bird customers. So, they sipped coffee and did a little of this, knowing that in a short while they would be busy with customers and the coffee would be forgotten. Jacqulyn and John arrived, and Melissa told Jacqulyn about the girl in the wheelchair. Jacqulyn glanced over at the girl but did not recognize her as someone she knew. She went over to the girl and said she was Jacqulyn. The girl said she knew her, but Jacqulyn did not know her. She laughed a pretty laugh and said that she was perfume man's secretary and she prepared paper for Jacqulyn and the perfume man to sign but she was always in the other room and never mingled with the customers. The girls assume that perfume man was probably averse to having an invalid in his employment as he didn't treat her with respect but was gruff and short with her. By then Jacqulyn realized who she was and remembered that it seemed odd that perfume man never let her talk to the girl, but he would go to the doorway and tell the girl what he wanted. One day Jacqulyn noticed the girl, but she was busy and didn't notice Jacqulyn looking at her. Jacqulyn also did not notice she was in a wheelchair in front of her. So, after the introduction, Jacqulyn said to go by the coffee table as she would like some coffee and she thought the girl could use a refill. Jacqulyn still had no idea why she was there but for some reason she thought it was urgent. She was too shy to explain her visit. Finally it came out that she was unemployed, and she heard that Jacqulyn was looking for a receptionist for the deodorant company. Her name was Ming Wu, and she had many years of experience. A closer look at the girl revealed that she was a young woman between thirty-five to forty years old. Sometimes it's hard to tell the age of certain nationalities. Miss Wu continued and said perfume man was in a psychiatric ward at the City Hospital. He was an alcoholic and he had diabetes and he also didn't take care of himself or his business and eventually, the bank foreclosed on his mortgage, so he was forced out of business. That happened over a year ago and she could not get work because she was in a wheelchair. Jacqulyn said she could use her and to start tomorrow and she noticed that she looked threadbare, so she asked Melissa to give her an advance of $300. The girl began to weep. Melissa asked how she got here, and she said she took buses. Jacqulyn and John drove her to Mario's, and they had breakfast and she was then driven home. To get to the red brick building would be easy for her as she lived on the same street that the red brick building was on.

The next day Jacqulyn met her and introduced her to her duties. She was to answer the telephone and greet people. The wheelchair was now in position with a little rearranging and Ming could easily wheel herself to the reception desk and talk to people. She asked her what her salary was and that she was grateful to have the job. Melissa call Jacqulyn and told her and Jacqulyn said to give her a top salary for the type of work that Ming was being asked to do.

She was confronted by a dark complexion man who said that he worked with Jacqulyn many years ago when she was employed with Constance and that his aunt hired him. He said he was a plant engineer in a bottling plant In Texas and would like a job if there was one available. Mr. Rock told her that a good plant engineer was worth his weight in gold. He and Darrell would be fine, but the proof would be in the pudding if there was a real calamity situation. Mr. Rock was at the deodorant building and told him about the plant engineer looking for work. Melissa figured the guy was lacking something as plant engineers did not grow on trees. *Did you ask if he had transportation because he was in the middle of something?* The man, whose name was Jack Sperry, said that he had a car and if he had an address, he would go to talk to Mr. Rock. She drew him a map and said it was about four blocks away. Melissa called Mr. Rock and said the man appeared to be well-educated and didn't smell of alcohol and didn't slur his words, but it would be up to Mr. Rock to make his decision.

Jack Sperry was at the plant about the time Melissa hung up. Mr. Rock had enough experience by now that by asking a few key questions he would know if the applicant was full of baloney and just looking for a paycheck to hold him over. Mr. Rock looked at him and said, "It shows you haven't worked for five years. Why?"

Jack figured he couldn't lie to Mr. Rock because he was all business, so Jack told him the truth. He said that he got into an accident that killed the lady passenger in the other vehicle. The passenger in his vehicle got hurt. He suffered severe leg problems and eventually they had to amputate his foot above the ankle. During the trial his wife's parents said that he wasn't drunk because he and his wife were going to be divorced but he said he didn't and never had a DUI or was ever involved in an accident. The accident occurred when a derelict stepped off the curb and started to cross the street, so he slammed on his brakes and the car following rear ended him. Normally the car in the rear that crashed into the car in front was liable for his own car and result, but the driver was a politician in Houston and the girl was a pickup. No one knew her name and she had no identification. "So, the jury found me guilty although they could not say I was drinking or under the influence of drugs. My employer gave the court a good recommendation for my work ethics, but I was found guilty and sentenced to ten years for involuntary manslaughter. I served five years and I'm out on probation for five years. I got out three days ago and read about your new plan so here I am. The whole case is a matter of public record so anyone can verify what happened."

Mr. Rock was impressed with the man's honesty and said he would verify his story, talk to his former employer and to come back in two days. If the man did not come back, Mr. Rock would write him off as a good try but that's all, but Mr. Jack Sperry did call him two days later to see what the verdict was. Mr. Rock said he would hire him at the prevailing wage, but he would be entered as a temporary worker for six months. Mr. Sperry was well pleased and asked Mr. Rock when he was to report to work. Mr. Rock said eight a.m. tomorrow. Mr. Sperry said he had all his own tools, that his a brother kept them safe for him, so he was good to go. Darrell was very happy to see Mr. Sperry because now he would have a very experienced man at the helm, and it would relieve some pressure off himself and Mr. Rock. It didn't take Mr. Rock long to evaluate Mr. Sperry as indispensable as he watched Mr. Sperry very closely. The product would justify its existence by public opinion. So, the product and package sure were locked together. If one failed, the other would. Sometimes as it happens things go too smoothly and that's how the term "calm before the storm" originated but there was no storm. The deodorant line now had five distinct products and the advertising budget was used to the maximum. One ad said, "Men are you man enough to Switch". Another was "Woman love men that Switched."

The studio was doing so well Jacqulyn was getting calls to sell or merge. She was also getting calls to list on the stock exchange and to explore an I. P. O. That would include the Switch deodorant line and Constance's studio, but John and Jacqulyn said no for now. Mr. Rock was in perfume and he knew the industry so he said that things probably had changed since his plant explosion. But if everything were equal, they hadd probably made a good decision to enter the perfume market. The whole third story of the red brick building was empty and could be an ongoing operation very easily. *But let's not rush. A lot of data would have to be digested.* One thing in Mr. Rock's favor was he still had all the original patent formulas of the Princess Perfume and he would produce products blindfolded as he was so familiar with the Princess product. The biggest hurdle would be installing another automated bottling plant which should be easier now that they had one plant already under their belt. Mr. Rock told John and Jacqulyn he would contact the engineer then install the switch plant as he bought and sold plants all the time.

John and Jacqulyn were facing a few major moves as we enter a new year. One, they both agreed that they had outlived their stay in John's family home. First, the cost to remodel would be high plus it would never achieve their needs. As the location of the house is not the most desirable, it would not behoove them to demolish the home and replace. So, the options are to rent the home or sell it. Jacqulyn had another idea: let Ming live in the home as she needs support more than the other staff members and she is doing an excellent job as a receptionist at Switch headquarters. So, John agreed the only hang up is: John and Jacqulyn had not been able to decide where they would live. John said that his realty firm had some outstanding possibilities that were presently on the market, and they could purchase some undeveloped property. So, the conundrum continued to exist.

The second big decision facing the two was the decision on whether to move ahead with the perfume division. Mr. Rock was going to evaluate the present market and report to John and Jacqulyn his thoughts. Mr. Rock was in favor of entering that market as there was room for a quality fragrance entity, especially in the United States. Europe had always been the number one fragrance market in the world, along with Paris. Mr. Rock also said that a bottling plant that was fully automatic could be installed and up and running in six months. The third decision: what to do with the penthouse. Jacqulyn's every sense told her to remodel the penthouse and live there but John seemed to think that it was too close to the activity. John's idea was to buy away from everything so when they went home, they went home to forget business. John's idea was segregation — separate the two worlds so that one can live.

John would like several acres in a quiet setting building — a comfortable home having a swimming pool, a tennis court — an outdoor living, maybe a couple of horses.

Jacqulyn looked at him in amazement. John had never had what he thought he wanted. John's world was twenty-four hours of business— sell homes, sell properties, sell businesses. *I can't see my husband floating around in a pool with a glass of champagne and the music blaring. Nor can I imagine myself doing the same. I yearn for that day when I struggled every minute of every day to live for myself and Shelly. No, I have so much but I have nothing. John has so much but he has nothing. Same with Mr. Rock and Eric. At one time money was everything, now achievement is everything. Could we just sell everything and try to be normal? I don't know. What I do know is that we are not normal when all we do is live for another day to make money. John suggests we buy a home that's compatible to what we want and if we decide to build, we could always sell. That's John's mentality and always will be. He'll buy more, sell, buy, or move. As I am sitting contemplating everything and nothing John calls.* He said that Mario wanted to sell the restaurant and for me to set a price. Mario also said that Hans, his cook, was very interested in buying the restaurant. Hans had been a good employee and he had saved his money his whole life. Also, he got some money and property from an inheritance. We'd like to see Hans buy the restaurant. So, John would set a price and discuss with Mario and his aunt as to the feasibility of his determined figure. Mario, like so many small businesses that never really were big time, made some money and lived well so he did better than most pop and mom ventures. John understood Mario's position. John and Antonia were getting up in age and Antonia has had a harder time lately — working really serious — but the long hours, mental fatigue and daily grinding were taking a toll on Antonia and Mario's life. So, he says *God forbid something happens to my Antonia. I would die.* Old timers thought that way mostly. Many old-timer folks never hit the jackpot, but they were satisfied to struggle and maintain their status quo for the love of each other and for their children. Although Mario and Antonia had a very modest amount of savings, they did have the restaurant and their small home was paid for. John and Jacqulyn offered to give them money as they now had so much, but Mario ws a proud man and would not accept charity.

That evening John and Jacqulyn discussed the day's events. So, Jacqulyn said that if John agreed, this is what she would like to do. First, John would buy a nice comfortable house in a decent neighborhood and because he had so much experience in the realty business, she knew he would do the right thing. *When we move, we will try to help Ming as we previously discussed. We will proceed with the perfume and you will notify Mr. Rock to buy the machinery. You and I will explore buying bottles and labels and set up an advertising campaign. I think it should be a complete separate business from the Switch deodorant business. We must name the product. That will be a make-or-break decision that the public will buy. I love the Princess Perfume business, but Mr. Rock said no. The buyers of products like perfume have a very long memory and Princess Perfume hurt a lot of buyers not because of the product but because of the circumstances arisen from the explosion.*

Jacqulyn thought of the name Amour and John liked it. Jacqulyn was proud as she really had made a significant impact since Shelly, but John and everyone else thought differently. But in one second she changed her attitude towards herself. Amour would be passed around to the staff for opinions. "Remember, just because I said Amour, it doesn't mean it should be the ultimate name as an angle last forever, but we will be gone."

Mr. Rock thought the name Amour was striking as the association to love was what perfume was all about. The work on floor three started. The one big favorable problem was the way floor one and two would not be impacted with dust and disruptiveness of any sort while floor three was being prepared. The engineer called Mr. Rock and assured him the deal for the bottling plant had been struck and as soon as it closed escrow he would start dismantling and run to the red brick building where he would begin setting up the plant. Mr. Rock was pleased. The floor space was to be divided as such: the plant took up a good portion, the conveyor belts, billing, and labeling apparatus covered a lot of territory At the end of the assembly was the packaging and shipping. There would be a space allowed for the chemistry lab which needed stainless steel tables and stainless steel shelving, sinks of different sizes, perfect lighting and completely fire-resistant floors, walls, and ceilings. The added costs would be minimized by the lowering of the insurance premium. In case of a fire explosion, it would be confined to that space and not the whole third floor or the whole building for that matter. There were offices and cubicles for staff. The one enormous cavity, the third floor, now seemed cramped, but it was conceived professionally by Mr. Rock and the designers. Day in and day out there were noises and bangs. At the end, everything came together, and they had achieved what they wanted. The remodel was almost over. The big thing now was for Mr. Rock to produce a lot of products. Mr. Rock bought twenty large stainless barrels like the wood barrel that the wineries used. Darrell was available to help him as the engineer had his own experience crew. So, Mr. Rock and Darrell produced perfume products — the same ones that he produced years ago at Princess Perfume. Only now it was called Amour perfume.

Mr. Rock tried to keep it a secret that Princess was Amour. If that got around then it would be like swapping a big label across Amour saying: formally Princess. Even Darrell did not know. Only Mr. Rock, Jacqulyn, John, and Melissa were privy to that confidential bit of history. Well, Mr. Rock and Darrell feverishly worked on the actual product. John and Jacqulyn were busy talking to advertisers and promoting people and talking to artists who created fantastic labels for everything from a can of tomatoes to what John and Jacqulyn wanted. They also had to find a bottle as the appearance of the bottle and label sold the perfume as much as the perfume itself. John and Jacqulyn were familiar faces to these people as Jacqulyn ordered thousands of bottles for the Switch line. It might be just a bit bulkier and not as feminine. So, Jacqulyn went to the desk that said Mrs. Thompson. Mrs. Thompson and Jacqulyn did business together many times. John was introduced to Mrs. Thompson who got chairs for them, and they began. Mrs. Thompson said that the leak was out that a new perfume was on the horizon. Mrs. Thompson went on as she knew Jacqulyn and there were many perfumes from one dollar to two hundred dollars to infinity.

"So, if you have a perfume that strikes the fancy of women, you can set your own price and it will sell. Of course, you and John both know that, so let's sell you some bottles. Before we begin going through catalogs or such, let me tell you a story. About six months ago, a guy came in here to talk bottles. Incidentally, he was a perfume manufacturer somewhere. In Italy I think it was. He had a briefcase that contained four or five of the most fashionable bottles I have ever seen. He said he needed some bottles to copy his bottles and keep the process or whatever they used confidential. After the initial order he would order essentially more or less fifty-thousand bottles per order. So, the order was placed. We created the model and manufactured fifty thousand. Quite a coupe for this old lady and we got a nice deposit. We created the mold and manufactured his fifty-thousand bottles then a funny thing happened. We never heard a word from him again. We tried contacting his firm and we got a blank. So there you have it — the fiasco of my life. Unless someone wants that bottle, we have a big investment in producing the mold and we have fifty thousand bottles.

Now Jacqulyn, you know me well enough that if I told you this bottle will sell perfume you would have to accept that as a fact. Plus, if you like the bottle, I will give you fifty percent off ,plus you would have exclusive use of the molds and I mean exclusive."

So, Mrs. Thompson opened the bottom drawer of her desk and brought out this exquisite bottle that was wrapped in a special cloth used by bottlers. Jacqulyn was amazed as the bottle was beautifully designed and very feminine looking. It was exactly what was needed to launch the product. Jacqulyn said she would take the lot but would need to fit a label to the bottle. Mrs. Thompson handed her the bottle and said her word was good. If a label could be fitted to the bottle, the sale was guaranteed.

Incidentally her realtor John was also impressed with the model. Jacqulyn told John when they reached the car that this little gem was going to sell Amour. The artist at the label shop said it was no problem so he took photos of the bottle and quickly cut out different label shapes. He told Jacqulyn and John to come back in a week and he would have samples for them to look at. So, Jacqulyn told him the name of the perfume and they left. Jacqulyn was very anxious to show the bottle to Mr. Rock. Mr. Rock was flabbergasted. All he could say was, "Wow, the gods are with you."

So, Jacqulyn gave Mr. Rock the bottle and told him to show it to the engineer. The engineer looked at it and said, "Cute little thing. No problem on my end. Just let me know that this is it and I'll do the rest, be assured."

Mr. Rock laughed. Setting up the plant was hard but it was the easiest part. It was an art to fit the whole system to a bottle that was so small then adapt the whole system again to say a pint or quart but that was what the engineer was paid the big bucks for.

Jacqulyn followed up on the label and John was free, so they went to lunch and then to the printing shop. The artist promised he had six stereotypes ready. Some were straight lines and some were more decorative, but they all looked good. It was going to be a chore trying to decide. Jacqulyn asked the artist if he had a duplicate plate so that he could preview them with others. He told her he would make a copy in a few minutes which he did. The first preview was with Mrs. Thompson, and she was not much help as she said they were all excellent.

"Just close your eyes and point," she said. Of course she was trying to be funny but when you consider the bottles and labels, it better be right. Kelly was modeling so she didn't see them. Mr. Rock said that they were all good but if he had to choose one, it would be this one. Jacqulyn said she would like to take her to the Switch building as she wanted to get Ming's idea. She said she wasn't very artistic but if she bought some perfume, it would be the product that she would be concerned with, but all the labels were very attractive. Just then Mr. Engineer came strolling into the lobby and he greeted everyone and said he had a tough day. So, Jacqulyn excused herself and asked him to pick a label. He picked the one Mr. Rock picked. So Jacqulyn said if they're all good and two were picked by two different lookers, that was the one they would use. So that was decided.

John drove Jacqulyn to the label shop and Jacqulyn ordered the fifty-thousand bottles — to be delivered when she requested. She also wanted in writing that the molds were the property of Amour perfume. Mrs. Thompson said she would have the attorneys draw up the agreement. They went to see the artist and congratulated him on a job well done and this was their choice. So fifty thousand labels were ordered. Jacqulyn hired three different marketing agencies to promote Amour. She also had special salespeople who contacted department stores, dress shops, and beauty shops to see if they could get advance orders and precious shelf space.

Amour was launched and Mr. Rock was as proud as a new daddy because Amour was his baby. The initial reaction was very positive, and John and Jacqulyn and Mr. Rock and Melissa went out for surf and turf at a local restaurant. Mr. Rock said he wanted a side dish of prawns. So, they all had their fill of prawns and filet mignon. Life was good.

Six months went by and the sky fell on Mr. Rock. The studio was doing extremely well. Switch was doing two times the volume projected. Amour was setting sale records. They were all cash cows. Jacqulyn was getting offers from the biggest Wall Street corporations to merge and sell outright to go public but she held that. *It's only money and if we sell out, we'll be like Mr. Rock — millions in the bank but you can only eat so many prawns. If you have been conservative all your life, how you could spend indiscriminately? You can't. People think it's easy, but it isn't.*

Jacqulyn could buy any car at any price and if she was so inclined, but she still drove Constance's Lincoln. She washed it, she polished it and she thought the world of that car. Getting back to Mr. Rock, Eric Crawford was a big player. Eric Crawford's father was wealthy beyond comprehension in Texas. He was never really in politics, but the present administration wanted him to be the ambassador to France, so he accepted. Mr. Crawford always took Eric with him when he and his wife went to France now that he was ambassador. Crawford needed to buy a home and reside in Paris. Eric went to school in Paris and after finishing, he attended college, but he fell in love with art. He was not an artist, but he learned the act of analyzing and appraising art. He was a very young, devoted student of art and at an early age he went to work for the largest auction house in Paris. They auctioned 50% of all the art produced by artists. They had a large staff of expert appraisers as the world art was struck with fraud. This was the world of art. Everyday, people were sent to jail or prison because they thought they could beat the system. So, the auctioneer house was forced to protect their reputations and hire appraisers to verify every painting that was auctioned. They had to guarantee that. An authenticpainting was worth one million dollars and whatever the buyer deemed his price. He was one of the youngest appraisers to reach the title of master appraiser. After working for the auction house for several years, Eric decided to go into the art appraisal field as a free agent. So, young Eric left the employ of the auction house. He was well known for his dedication and honesty, so he was always in demand by auction houses, art studios, and museums. Museums often inherited millions of dollars' worth of art each year. Museums often put prices on the pieces that were on display. The museum had to have insurance on all their art, so the appraisal determined how much insurance was needed to cover each piece of art. So frequently Eric was called in before a showing to verify art that might have been appraised years before. So, the museums were constantly upgrading their art sections to keep up with inflation or other factors that influenced appraisals.

Eric was appraising some art for this museum that was going to have a showing and he noticed a girl looking at a wall of art. She wasn't beautiful but she wasn't hard to look at. He introduced himself. She said her name was Melissa and they talked about their personal ambitions. Melissa was very candid and said her ambition was to become an artist but early on she knew it was told that she was good enough to probably come out a good living, but she would never attain star status, so she decided to learn all about appraising as she wanted to be in the field of art. There actually were no schools to learn appraising or very few of them.

The appraisers learned by studying appraised paintings and putting their own price on the paintings. If the painting was appraised at one-thousand dollars and the aspiring appraiser would come close to the one thousand dollars, they were on the right track. Eric asked Melissa if he could take her to dinner and she agreed. One thing led to another, and the one dinner was repeated so it could be called more than just a casual thing. It became a rather torrid affair. Just as quickly as it began, it ended. Melissa disappeared with no word or explanation. Eric hired private detectives to trace her. The closest he came to was when the detective said there was a sighting of a girl of her description in Italy. It was to be ten years later that Eric and Melissa met again. By this time, Eric had moved to New York City and opened a large art studio called Eric's Art Studio. It eventually was known as the in place for art and artists. Eric appraised art sold and held art shows. One of the artists that probably made Eric more famous was Constance. She sold all her paintings through Eric. They were very close but never more than that. Constance was self-sufficient so early in her artist life. She began to feel like many artistic people — that each painting was a part of them. They could not see selling but most painters or artists were not self-sufficient, so they painted to make a living. Eric was in New York City for several years.

One day Eric looked up and standing in the doorway was Melissa. It was as if she had just stepped out for a moment, but it was ten years. Melissa looked maybe a little more beautiful, maybe looked a little younger. Her figure was the same. Eric ran to her and grabbed her hand. It had been ten years. *Could he have the audacity to hug and kiss her?* He thought not. He welcomed her into the studio. She remarked how good he looked and thought the studio was the best. Eric asked about her disappearance and why. She said if he had a cup of coffee, she would tell him the whole ten years story. The studio was used to Eric being there one minute and not the next. So when he told Alice said he would be tight up for a while she thought nothing of it. He asked Alice to bring them a tray of coffee and some cookies. Eric let Melissa into his office. He was in a daze. It was not like Eric to lose it. Coffee arrived. She was trying to get her thoughts together. Eric was watching her closely to see if she trembled drinking the coffee. In other words, *was she sick? Something had to bring her here but what?*

She said that the day she left she knew she had to leave because all she could think of was Eric. She couldn't focus on anything and she was drained emotionally. She was like a zombie. "I couldn't paint or concentrate I was stifled. I had just sold a painting for one hundred or so and I had a few dollars, so I decided to leave. I drove you to the little office you had and went home — put the car keys on the table and took a bus to the train station. Didn't dare call you for fear I would get cold feet and not leave. When I was younger, I lived in a villa that was used for displaced people, mostly children. My parents were both deceased, so I was placed there. While I was there, I learned to paint, and I was like a teacher to some of the children. I was there a year and a half. One day, the mistress called me into her office she said that she got a call from a friend that needed an artist teacher and possibly an appraiser. It was a small museum near Rome. Then she said that if she could be frank with her, she would continue. So, she said that my artist talents were good but not of star quality. If I continued as an artist, I probably would make a fair living but that was it. So, she suggested that I concentrate on appraising as there was a demand for good appraisers. She said that my paintings were good enough, that I should not abandon the painting as it would probably get better and better and could bring in some serious money. So, I accepted the new job. It proved to be a good choice. I was there for one and one-half years. Also I learned quite a bit about art in general and the nuances of appraising. She was a professor of art in Rome before coming to the museum. The bottom fell out of the economy and the board said that they would have to tighten their belts, so everyone got laid off. When I first got there, the staff was the lady that hired me plus a professional artist gone to drink but was very good when sober. Then I was hired as a junior artist appraiser. They helped an art class one day a week and I was a filling teacher practically every week, again because of a drinking problem with the teacher. She was doing it as charity. One day, I went to visit a small art studio. The proprietor was a hunched back old man who seemed really alert but deformed. He did not have what I wanted but he did have some strong coffee and biscotti and he invited me to join him. We talked and I told him I painted a little and appraised less. So, he said that he didn't have enough money to buy my art but asked if I wanted to put it in the studio. He called the shop and said if it sold, he would take a small cut — sort of like consignment. So that's what I did. He had an old desk that I cleaned up and I put a small sign on the desk that read Artist/Appraiser. Now I was a freelancer. Of course, I was never there because of my job at the museum but if something came up, he would call me. Surprisingly there were calls and I was making more than my salary at the museum. I don't know where the leads were coming from, but I took them as they came. That went on for five years, but Pedro died, and the heirs liquidated the shop and that was the end of that. A year or so before Pedro died, the repeat of what happened at the other museum occured. They released all the staff because of money. I was fortunate to have the old man

Pedro and his shop to sustain me. Rome was twenty miles away so I took a train and went there to see about employment but there was none. So, I did the only logical thing and bought a ticket on a boat and came to America. I wasn't an American citizen. My mother was from Ohio where I was born, but shortly after I was born, she moved to Italy where she passed on. I lived in the house for homeless children which is another name for the orphanage. Eric, it was my love for you that made this happen. So now I've grown up a bit since then and maybe a bit smarter as time will tell. So, if you want to hear the truth, I am looking for work, not charity but something I can link with and feel good again as it's been over a year that Mr. Pedro's job was over."

Eric didn't hesitate. He said I could start tomorrow at eight a.m. "Start as a salesperson and we would go forward from there."

He pulled out his wallet and gave me one thousand dollars. At dinner that evening, our affair ten years ago was like it never was put on hold. Eric and I were not meant to be husband and wife. Interesting years — we lived together, and we would part ways and come together again — never together but never apart. He would do anything for me, and I, too, for him. We both loved each other but that was it for the thirty odd years we knew each other.

Amy came to Constance's studio D Art as a young artist andsalesperson. She developed into an indispensable part of Constance's studio. Darrell was hired by Mr. Rock as an apprentice chemist and he was good, but he lacked the spark to exploit his talent. He would always be ultra-reliable and always did his job well. He didn't drink or smoke or play around. he was too good to be true. Darrell made good money and with the aid of Amy, they never had to look back. Amy and Darrell married. Amy was on the verge of being a mother. Kelly was a good friend of Shelly's. They both were budding models. Kelly came to work for Constance as an in-store model and she filled in as a salesperson. Kelly sold more art than the other salespeople. She was very pretty and always in demand as a model. Melissa loved her and Amy. Mr. Rock was a professional chemist. He knew the game inside and out. Mr. and Mrs. Rock founded perfume and the product was destined to be a big-time player in the perfume industry when he had a big step back when an explosion occured in a chemist shop occupying a space below him. That ultimately put him out of business. His wife passed on and eventually he succeeded to get back from his insurance company what was due him. He invested his money wisely and became a multi-millionaire. He was devoted to Jacqulyn, a former employee of Princess Perfume. She was eighteen years old then. Jacqulyn subsequently fell into good times and she and her sister were going to be manufacturing male deodorant. Mr. Rock, being a chemist, made deodorant a dream come true. After the explosion Jacqulyn had a very rough time as she was the sole support of her younger sister. But fortune again befell her, and she was the principal beneficiary to Constance's art collection which exceeded two-hundred art pieces. Eric was instrumental in helping Jacqulyn set up Constance's Studio D Art and Eric brought Jacqulyn and Melissa together. Melissa was the appraiser and manager of Constance's Art Studio. Melissa and Mr. Rock were a twosome. Mr. Rock planned on marrying Melissa, but Eric spoiled his dream after Melissa and Eric met again. Eric and Melissa got married and Mr. Rock was devastated. He ingested some of his chemicals and committed suicide. He couldn't live without Melissa. When Melissa went to New York and saw Eric, she knew that she always loved him. After thirty years, they were definitely in love. The only thing was that Melissa lived in Chicago and Eric in New York City. So, they decided to get married and stay in New York.

John and Jacqulyn were wealthy beyond comprehension. In John's case he was always one of the top people in the Premier Realty firms in Chicago. So, John, with his vitality and modern approach to business, brought the firm to where it was now. Jacqulyn's story was a rags-to-riches story. When John and Jacqulyn decided to sell,

Eric and Melissa stepped in and purchased Constance's art studio and decided to let Amy manage the art studio. They lived in New York where their love for art was still being pursued. An operation in Europe bought the deodorant and perfume business so now the two of them were unemployed, former businesspeople. Could they survive living the life of luxury? Time will tell.

THE END

www.ingramcontent.com/pod-product-compliance
Lightning Source LLC
LaVergne TN
LVHW011951070526
838202LV00054B/4893